PULP Literature

PULP LITERATURE PRESS
Issue No. 42, Spring 2024

Publisher: Pulp Literature Press; Editor-in-Chief: Jennifer Landels; Senior Editor: Mel Anastasiou; Acquisitions Editor: Genevieve Wynand; Poetry Editors: Daniel Cowper & Emily Osborne; Assistant Editors: Brooklynn Hook, Sierra Louie, Ellen Spacey; Copy Editor: Amanda Bidnall; Proofreader: Sierra Louie; Graphic Design: Amanda Bidnall & Sierra Louie; Cover Design: Kate Landels; Subscriptions: Carol McCauley; For advertising rates, direct inquiries to info@pulpliterature.com.

Cover painting, *Red Planet Raygunne and the Answer to Everything* by Mel Anastasiou. Illustrations for 'High Reward' by Gabriel Craven and Mikayla Fawcett. All other illustrations by Mel Anastasiou.

Pulp Literature: ISSN 2292-2164 (Print), ISSN 2292-2172 (Digital), Issue No. 42, Spring 2024.

Published quarterly by Pulp Literature Press, 21955 16 Ave, Langley, BC, Canada V2Z 1K5, pulpliterature.com, at $18.00 per copy. Annual subscription $60.00 in Canada, $80.00 in continental USA, $92.00 elsewhere. Printed in Surrey, BC, Canada, by Fraser Printers Ltd. Copyright © 2024 Pulp Literature Press. All stories and works of art copyright © 2024 their authors as per bylines.

Pulp Literature Press is based in the unceded traditional Coast Salish Territories of the Katzie, Kwantlen, Matsqui, and Semiahmoo First Nations.

Pulp Literature Press gratefully acknowledges the support of the Canada Council for the Arts and the Government of Canada.

Pulp Literature is a proud member of the Magazine Association of BC and Magazines Canada.

TABLE OF CONTENTS

FROM THE PULP LIT PULPIT

Our Universe, Ourselves

As we embark on the literary journey that is Issue 42 of our beloved magazine, we can't resist the temptation to pay homage to the cosmic wit of Douglas Adams and his magnum opus, *The Hitchhiker's Guide to the Galaxy*. Of course, the Answer to the Ultimate Question of Life, the Universe, and Everything, remains a mystery.

But in life and the very best of stories, isn't that sometimes the way? Back here on planet *Pulp*, we love work that reminds us of the serendipity, coincidence, and interconnectedness of all things — those literary adventures that invite us to suspend disbelief and venture into worlds (galaxies?) where the ordinary becomes extraordinary, where the mundane becomes magical.

Questions without answers; answers without questions. If we're up for it, that's where we find the room to explore, ponder, and play in the delicious uncertainties of being human. And in these pages, there's a controlled — dare we say — chaos in the variety of stories and voices, each of which beautifully captures a small corner of the cosmos.

So, dear readers, immerse yourself in the magic, embrace the absurd, revel in the uncertainty, and delight in the infinite possibility of life, the universe, and everything. After all, the journey, literary and otherwise, is surely as important as the destination. And the answer may very well be found right here, in 42.

Happy reading, fellow cosmic travellers!

~Genevieve Wynand

In THIS ISSUE

Red Planet Raygunne and the Answer to Everything by **Mel Anastasiou** pays tribute to Douglas Adams and the literary adventures that await our readers

Travelling with us are dragons in Alberta's Rocky Mountains with 'La Vitesse' by feature author **Kelly Robson**, and ninjas in small-town Ontario and on the road to Tuktoyaktuk with 'The Newtonbrook Ninja' by **Preston Lang** and Jack Whyte Storytellers' Award winner 'The Ice Road' by **Trish Gauntlett**.

Along for the ride are meddling ghosts and workaday zombie-hunters, with the opening chapters of *Take My Hand* by **Mel Anastasiou** and 'High Reward' from **Gabriel Craven** and **Mikayla Fawcett**.

We pick up some friends, frenemies, and migrant children along the way, with 'Masquerade' by **Wiley Wei-Chiun Ho**, a new instalment of *The Shepherdess* by **JM Landels**, Raven Contest winner 'Neverender' by **Krista Jane May**, and 'Octavier' by **Nat Kishchuk**.

And rounding out the journey, we've got primal horror with 'Flehmen Grimace' and 'Watercolours', both from **EC Dorgan**, and a trio of sharp and glittering poems from **Leanne Boschman**, **Pattie Palmer-Baker**, and **Marri Champié**, the winners of our inaugural Kingfisher Poetry Prize.

LA VITESSE

Kelly Robson

Kelly Robson *grew up in the foothills of the Rockies and now lives in downtown Toronto. Her novelette* A Human Stain *won the 2018 Nebula Award, and her short fiction won the 2022, 2019, and 2016 Aurora Awards. She has also been a finalist for the Hugo, Nebula, World Fantasy, Theodore Sturgeon, Locus, Astounding, Aurora, and Sunburst Awards. She is the author of the short fiction collection* Alias Space *and the novellas* Gods, Monsters, and the Lucky Peach *and* High Times in the Low Parliament. *'Good for Grapes' was the feature story for* Pulp Literature *Issue 23, Summer 2019, and now we're delighted to bring you 'La Vitesse', which first appeared in* The Book of Dragons *(Jonathan Strahan, ed, 2020).*

$\mathscr{L}$A VITESSE

March 2, 1983, 30 kilometres southwest of Hinton, Alberta

"Rosie," Bea said under her breath, but the old school bus's wheels were rumbling over gravel, and her daughter didn't hear. Rosie was slumped in the shotgun seat, eyes closed. She hadn't moved since Bea had herded her onto *La Vitesse* at six-fifteen that morning. She wasn't asleep, though. A mother could always tell.

Bea raised her voice to a stage whisper. "Rosie, we got a problem."

Still no reaction.

"Rosie. Rosie. Rosie."

Bea snatched one of her gloves from the bus's dashboard and tossed it. Not at her kid—never at her kid; it bounced off the window and landed in Rosie's lap.

"Mom. I'm sleeping." Big scary scowl. Bea hadn't seen her kid smile since she'd turned fourteen.

"There's a dragon right behind us," she said silently, mouthing the words. None of the other kids had noticed, and Bea wanted to keep it that way.

Rosie rolled her eyes. "I don't read lips."

"A dragon," she whispered. "Following us."

"No way." Rosie bolted upright. She twisted in her seat and looked back through the central aisle, past the kids in their snowsuits and toques. "I can't see it."

The rear window was brown with dirty, frozen slush. Thank god. If the kids saw the dragon, they'd be screaming.

"Come here and look."

Rosie crawled out of her seat and leaned over her mother, hanging tight to the grab bar behind Bea's head. Her too-tight black parka carried a whiff of cigarettes.

Bea flipped open her window and adjusted the side-view mirror for Rosie. Behind the bus, a long, matte-black wing beat the air in a furious rhythm. The pale winter sun glinted on the silver scales that marked the wing's fore-edge.

"Wow," Rosie said, her voice so low it was almost a growl.

Bea stepped on the gas. *La Vitesse* surged ahead, revealing the dragon's broad chest rippling with flexed muscles. It lifted its taloned forelegs, as if reaching for the bus, and showed them the barest glimpse of a lissom neck and triangular, snake-like head before it caught up to the bus and disappeared into the mirror's blind spot.

Rosie pushed her ragged bangs out of her eyes and leaned closer to the mirror.

"No fire. Why isn't it trying to roast us?"

"I don't know. Maybe it's breathing too hard," Bea said. "But honey, you got to help me. Herd the kids into the front seats. Pack them in tight."

Rosie wasn't listening, though. She stared at the mirror, transfixed, watching the dragon's wing flexing from hooked tip to thick shoulder.

"Rose, please." Bea slapped the wheel with both hands. "Get the kids up front."

"Yeah, okay." Rosie straightened, then leaned over her mother again for one last look.

Even Bea had to admit her kid looked scary, especially lately, with her death metal T-shirts and her angry slouch. Not yet sixteen, but so big and tall she looked twenty. Add all that to the black eyeliner Rosie melted with a match and applied smouldering, and the spiky haircut she'd given herself in grade ten and kept short with Bea's only pair of good scissors, and yeah, Bea could understand why other mothers gave her hell for letting her kid look so rough.

Bea couldn't do anything about it. Rosie had always been more trouble than Bea could handle. But as long as she came home on the bus with Bea every day, nothing else mattered.

But Bea didn't like the way her daughter looked at the dragon. She wasn't scared, not even a bit. Maybe she was even glad to see it.

Bea drove the longest and most remote bus route in the school district. Starting at her trailer south of Cadomin, she headed north and picked up kids along the Forestry Trunk Road all the way past Luscar and the Cardinal River coal mine, then turned east on the Yellowhead Highway and hauled the kids through town to drop them off at all three schools.

The round trip took five hours—two and a half each way. *La Vitesse* was a fast bus with a big V8 engine, but Bea drove slow. She had to. The Forestry Trunk Road was gravel, heavily corrugated with washboard created by runoff from the surrounding mountains. The soft shoulders on either side of the gravel road could easily pull a vehicle into the ditch or off a cliff, and moose lurked around every corner—often right in the middle of the road. Bea had seen what hitting a big bull moose could do to a bus, and she didn't want anything to do with it.

So Bea drove slow. She was kind, too. School bus drivers were allowed to leave kids behind if they weren't waiting by the road on time, but Bea never did. Bears were common fall and spring, and cougars hunted year-round. A kid waiting for the bus made a nice warm snack.

And lately, Bea worried about dragons, too.

Rosie herded the kids into the front rows, three and four to a seat. Too rough; Rosie was always too rough with other kids, but it didn't matter now.

"We're playing a game," Bea sang out in her best sunny voice and smiled into the rearview mirror. "Let's see how fast *La Vitesse* can stop. I'll honk my horn ten times. You all count with me. On the tenth honk, I'll hit the brakes. Everyone hang on tight. Brace yourselves, okay?"

In the rearview, hoods and toques framed twenty pairs of big, scared eyes. They knew something was wrong. Kids always did.

"It'll be fun," she said, smiling wider. "Ready?"

The kids counted along as she honked. She hoped the horn might drive the dragon off, but she'd already tried that and it hadn't worked.

On the tenth honk, they were on a good flat straightaway. Decent gravel, no potholes or washboard. Shallow ditches on either side, lined with slender young spruce. If *La Vitesse* skidded off the road, they'd be okay. The bus would stick, though. Bea had faith.

When she slammed on the brakes, one kid screamed. Several whimpered. The dragon hit the back of the bus with a hollow *thunk. La Vitesse* skidded but stayed square in the middle of the road. Bea shifted to first gear and slammed the gas. *La Vitesse's* engine roared, then screamed. Bea let the revs build and shifted to second, her foot flat on the floor.

In the side-view, the dragon lay crumpled on the gravel, wings canted like a broken tent.

Bea held her breath, flicking her gaze from road to mirror to road. Dead, she hoped. Let it be dead.

The dragon lifted its head and yawned. A tongue of blue flame licked from between its fangs. It clawed the gravel with the hinges of its wings and staggered to its feet. In the early morning light, its eyes sparked a keen and murderous ice white.

Bea had seen the first dragon in 1981, two years back, when she was bringing home a bus full of soccer players after a tournament in Jasper.

She'd been cruising east along the Athabasca River, heading toward the Jasper park gates. The sunset light turned the mountains mellow orange, and the trees threw long, spear-shaped shadows across the highway. *La Vitesse's* speedometer was two fingers below the speed limit. The wheels hummed on the gently curving highway. Bea was thinking about making barbecue ribs for Sunday supper when she spotted the dragon perched on the massive cliff edge of Roche Miette.

On the mountain high above the highway, the dragon's red scales gleamed bloody in the sun. It stretched its wings and beat them once, then pointed its narrow head at the highway below. It dropped off the cliff, kited low, and disappeared behind the trees.

When *La Vitesse* rounded the curve, the red dragon hunched, spread-winged, atop the dynamite-blasted rock face where mountain met highway, a bighorn sheep clamped in its jaws.

"Look," Bea squeaked. But the kids were making too much noise to hear. She floored the gas and watched the dragon recede in the rearview mirror. If she busted the speed limit all the way home, nobody noticed.

Twenty kids, and Rosie made twenty-one. The youngest not yet six, and Rosie the oldest at nearly sixteen. More than half of them were crying.

"Brake check all done!" Bea's voice was high with tension. She hunched in her seat and twisted from side to side, scanning the sky through the side-view mirrors. "The brakes are fine! *La Vitesse* is a good bus."

She patted the dashboard like it was a horse.

"Mom. They heard it hit us," Rosie growled. "Fucking tell them."

"A moose ran up the ditch," Bea said. "Gave us a little knock on the bum, but we're fine."

The kids wailed louder. Tony Lalonde yanked his toque down over his eyes and howled.

"The moose is fine, too," Bea insisted. "Everything's okay."

But it wasn't okay. The dragon wasn't hurt. It flew a dozen car lengths behind, wings beating hard, mouth gaping. On every down stroke, that blue flame licked the road. Was it hot enough to melt her tires? Probably. She couldn't afford to find out.

Behind her, Rosie stood in the aisle, surfing the bumps. When the dragon tore the emergency exit off its hinges and lunged up the aisle, Rosie would be its first victim. It would rip her daughter's head off and slaughter the kids one by one while Bea sat behind the wheel. She had to think of something.

"Rosie, honey," she said in the sweetest voice she could muster. "Come and drive the bus."

When Bea had reported the red dragon to the Hinton RCMP, the Mountie at the front desk just smiled.

"Imagination goes wild in the mountains," he said. "I had a coal miner in here the other day saying a giant black cat was lurking around his dragline."

"Yeah, okay, but have you been to Jasper lately?" Bea asked. "You know the bighorn sheep along the highway? The ones that graze under Roche Miette? They're gone. All of them."

The Mountie smirked. "Last summer a bunch of campers said they saw a Bigfoot at Jarvis Lake."

Bea gave up. He was from Toronto. What did he know? Nothing.

Bea and her family weren't coal miners, and they sure weren't campers. The mountains weren't terra incognita to her. She'd been born in the bush like her parents, and their parents, and so on back all the generations. Her ancestors lived in Jasper before it was a park, until they were kicked out and resettled in Cadomin. Those Rocky Mountain ranges were her true home, so when Bea said she saw a dragon, she saw it. No matter what some Mountie said.

"You want me to drive *La Vitesse*?" Rosie said. "Are you fucking kidding?"

From the back of the bus came a high-pitched rasping sound, like metal on metal, and if Bea had been unsure, she wasn't any longer.

"I'm not kidding. Take the wheel, please."

They exchanged positions awkwardly. Bea's ample hips didn't leave much room, but Rosie slid in behind her. What mattered most—after staying on the road—was keeping pressure on the gas pedal. Bea hung from the grab rail and stretched to keep her toe on the pedal, like a swimmer testing the water.

"Let go, let go, I got it." Rosie dug her shoulder into her mother's hip, hard.

"Okay, honey. Keep it above fifty, even on the curves. Floor it on the straightaways. And if you see anyone coming, lean on the horn and don't let up." Bea grabbed the fire extinguisher from the stepwell. When she stood, Joan Cardinal glared at her from under her glossy black bangs.

"I'm going to tell on you," Joan said, fully thirteen and fierce.

"That's okay, honey. You do that." Bea cradled the fire extinguisher like a baby.

"Let's play another game. Here are the rules. Everybody stay in your seat. Don't get up. Hold tight to your seat buddies, stay quiet, and do everything I say. If you do, we'll stop at Dairy Queen on the last day before Easter break. My treat."

Every kid's mouth dropped open. Ice cream was the bus driver's secret weapon.

"Sundaes or cones?" asked Sylvana Lachance, ten years old and already a master of negotiation.

"That depends on how good you are." Bea gave them a big motherly smile. "Now take off your snowsuits."

Rosie only had her learner's license but she'd been driving since she was ten. Out in the bush, all kids drove early. She'd learned on Bea's rusty Chevy Blazer, a four-speed with a sticky clutch, and had been driving it with confidence for years. Maybe the Blazer was nothing like *La Vitesse*, but Bea had no choice. She couldn't do anything about the dragon while stuck in the driver's seat.

Bea knelt in the aisle and stuffed her own parka inside Michelle Arsenault's tiny pink snowsuit, then padded the legs and arms with all the toques and scarves within reach.

"Who's got meat in their lunch today? Anyone?" The kids shrank in their seats. "If you've got it, I want it."

Blair Tocher threw her his lunch bag. Bea ripped it open and tore through the plastic wrap with her fingernails. Peanut butter, that was fine. All animals liked that, right? She smeared the insides of the sandwich all over the snowsuit.

"Nobody's got baloney for lunch? Sausage? Spam?" She tried to sound normal, but her voice was high and shrill.

"Give her your lunches," came a growl from the driver's seat, where Rosie hunched over the wheel. "Do it or I'll take us into the ditch."

Bags rained on Bea's head. Pork sausage on thick home-made bread with mustard and a lick of golden syrup—that would be Manon Laroche's grandkids. Baloney and cheese on brown—could be anyone's. Cookies, apples, celery with Cheez Whiz, those all went inside. The meat she smeared on the outside, grinding the greasy dregs into the snowsuit's knit cuffs and fuzzy hood.

"Okay," Bea said. She hefted the snowsuit in one arm and grabbed the fire extinguisher with her other hand. Then *La Vitesse* hit a pothole and the whole world spun around her.

"Try steering around them, Rose," Bea called from the floor.

"We got a logging truck coming." Rosie's voice was strangely deep.

"The horn. Hit the horn, honey!" Bea scrambled up the aisle on all fours. "He's got a radio, he'll call for help."

She waved her arms as Rosie blasted the horn. High in the truck's cab, a man in a trucker hat and stubble. Sunglasses though it wasn't even full light yet. One hand on the wheel with fingers raised in a lazy wave while the other hand brought a white styrofoam coffee cup to his lips for a sip. The truck flashed by.

"Did it work?" Rosie asked.

Bea ran to the first empty row and dived for the side window. She pressed her forehead against the cold glass and watched the truck disappear around a curve.

"No," Bea said. "He wasn't looking."

She limped up the aisle.

"I didn't turn on the hazard lights." She reached around her daughter and flicked on the hazards. She hit the warning lights too, the big orange traffic flashers front and back. Then she turned to the kids and took a deep breath.

On her left and right, all twenty kids, their precious little upturned faces. Tear-stained. Some contorted in fear. Most blank with shock. Her fault. She'd failed them all.

"It's a dragon," she said. "A big one."

Hinton didn't have a real library. Technically, the high school library was open to the public during school hours, but the librarian had ideas about the kinds of people who should be allowed to walk through the door. And in grade eleven, Bea had been banned. That might be sixteen years ago but as far as she knew, she was still banned.

Still, Bea needed information, and the library was the only place to get it.

After talking to the Mountie, she'd parked her bus at the hockey arena and walked over the playing fields toward the high school. Across the road, the pulp mill's stink-stacks belched rotten-egg vapour that drifted over the high school in a yellow haze.

She slipped into the library, walked softly to the reference shelf on the back wall, and pulled out *Encyclopaedia Britannica* Volume D. The entry on dragons was subtitled 'mythological creature'. She examined the illustrations. Clearly her dragon was the European type. Its snaky head and batlike wings matched the picture.

In European myth, it said, dragons terrorized entire valleys. After eating all the sheep, they'd start eating children.

Sheep. The sheep in the picture were fairy-tale versions, white and fluffy — nothing like bighorn sheep, with their sleek brown fur and curling horns. But the sheep under Roche Miette were gone. Did that mean the children were next?

"Bea Oulette."

Bea slammed the encyclopaedia closed. Mrs English watched her over the edge of her reading glasses.

"You're not allowed in here," she said. "You're banned."

Bea slipped the book back on the shelf and padded toward the door, keeping her eyes low.

"High school was a long time ago," she said softly as she passed the check-out desk.

"Not for me," the librarian snarled. "Don't come back."

Bea stood on a bus seat, reached high, and yanked open the rooftop safety hatch. It popped up easily — Bea kept the hinges well oiled. She steadied herself with one hand on the hatch's open edge and put her foot on the seatback, holding the greasy, stuffed, and smeared snowsuit between her teeth. With both hands, she shoved the hatch fully open.

Still awkward, but steadier now as she poked her head and shoulders through. Her hair whipped her face.

The dragon kited behind the bus. It scrabbled at the roof with its forelegs, raking its talons along the metal, looking for purchase. It lost its grip and fell behind, twisted in the air, then extended its long neck and beat its wings hard to catch up again.

All along the roof, long shiny marks gashed the paint and road dust. It was only a matter of time before it hooked a talon into *La Vitesse*.

Bea yanked the stuffed snowsuit through the hatch.

"Here," she yelled. "Do you want dinner?" She held the snowsuit by its waist and danced it, the arms and legs flopping. She pitched it at the dragon, then grabbed the hatch handles and slammed the hatch closed.

"Floor it, Rosie," she yelled.

But *La Vitesse* was already moving fast, and the highway intersection was on the horizon. No choice, they had to turn.

Bea lunged up the aisle.

"Slow down, honey! You won't make the turn."

"It didn't work." Rosie had her eyes on the side mirror. She wasn't even watching the road.

"Slow down now!"

Bea grabbed Rosie's shoulder and tried to pull her from the seat. The bus swerved. Rosie hunched over the wheel, gripping it with both hands, knuckles white, her whole body tense.

"Get out of the seat." Bea's voice rose, high and shrill. "Rosie, get out now."

A ripping sound of nails on metal. A gash of sunlight appeared in the ceiling over the left rear seat.

"That's a problem," Rosie said in a low, ominous voice.

"Slow down or we'll flip," Bea pleaded.

Rosie nudged the speed down a little. Bea grabbed two armfuls of kids from the seats behind Rosie and pushed them into seats opposite.

"Everyone on the right side." No time to be gentle. She grabbed arms and shoulders — whatever she could get a grip on, and then leaned in, pressing a seat full of the littlest kids under her belly. "Hold tight."

A popping sound. Bea twisted to look. Just above the smeared rear window, three talons punctured the bus's roof. The window itself was dark. The dragon hung from the back of the bus.

"Sundaes," Bea shouted. "If we make this turn, I'll buy you all sundaes."

"Hot fudge," Rosie said, and swung the wheel.

When she was a teenager, Bea took books from the high school library. Not often. Not every book. Just the good ones. But it wasn't stealing, not at first. When she started, she'd bring the books back. That's how she got caught.

First day of grade eleven, she was returning the books she'd taken home for the summer. Her plan was to slip them onto a shelf in the morning, make herself scarce, then sneak back in the afternoon like she'd never been there. But the load was too heavy. The books tore through the paper bag and spilled across the library linoleum, right in front of Mrs English.

In the vice principal's office, Bea kept her eyes hooded and looked at the floor. Never confront them, that was the survival strategy. It's what her grandpa did when hunters crossed the ridge where he set up his sweat lodge. It's what her mother did when the grocery store manager followed her through the aisles. Eyes down, calm breaths, wait for them to lose interest.

Getting banned only kept her out of the library for a week. Mrs English wasn't always watching. The student volunteers didn't care, and best of all, nobody else seemed to know what Bea knew. To steal a library book, all you had to do was sandwich it between two other books, say a binder and a math textbook, and hold the stack horizontal as you walked through the exit door. Held flat, the magnetic strip wouldn't set off the detector.

So Bea still had all the books she wanted, even though Hinton had no place to buy them but the drugstore's rack of boring bestsellers. She stocked up. After getting roasted by Mrs English and the vice principal, she felt absolutely fine about it.

La Vitesse's rear wheels screeched as they skidded sideways over the gravel-coated asphalt at the Forestry Trunk Road intersection. One rear wheel parted from the ground. The chassis shivered like it was Bea's own flesh.

She clung to the seatbacks with her nails and wrapped her sneaker-clad foot around a seat strut. Under her belly, she pressed the littlest kids hard into their seat. As *La Vitesse* fish-tailed, the dragon's claws ripped through the roof—four jagged rents lengthening in a clockwise curve as the dragon swung like a pendulum. A wing slapped the left rear windows, once, twice. A foot scrabbled at the glass, talons clacking in rapid staccato.

Warm wet spread across the thigh of Bea's jeans. One of the little kids was peeing himself. The dragon hung from the bus's side, talon tips hooked into the window seals. Its head whipped back and forth like a flag, bashing *La Vitesse's* side windows.

Under Bea, Tony Lalonde wailed. But if he could cry, he could breathe, and that was all that mattered to Bea.

The bus spun onto the highway, skidded across the eastbound lanes, and spat gravel across the median. The dragon's maw opened in a scream, but instead of sound, there was a lick of blue fire, transparent, like the propane flame from Bea's camp stove. Then it lost its grip and fell. One talon dangled from the window, smearing ashy gore from its root.

Bea plunged up the aisle and scrabbled at her daughter's shoulders.

"Out of my seat, now," she demanded.

"This is almost over." Under the caked eyeliner, Rosie's narrowed gaze was flinty. "Take care of the kids. They hate me."

"Rosie. No."

"That's okay. I hate them, too."

No use. Bea had never been able to stand up to her daughter. But Rosie wasn't wrong. It was almost over. She turned to face the huddled kids.

"We're going to be fine." She gave them her best motherly smile. "Rose will drive us to the RCMP station. Five minutes."

Those little tear-streaked faces just about broke her heart. Theresa Lalonde held tight to her little brother. He sobbed into his big sister's sweater. Bea stooped over them.

"Did I hurt you, Tony? I'm so sorry."

"This is your fault," Theresa said. And she wasn't wrong. Bea had known about the dragons for months, and what had she done? Nothing.

"It's okay. Someone will rescue us," she said, but she knew it wasn't true.

Encyclopaedia Britannica **Volume D** was the first book Bea had stolen in sixteen years. She hadn't lost her touch. All she had to do was wait for Mrs English's smoke break. The teenage girls behind the check-out desk didn't look up when Bea walked in, or when she took the volume off the reference shelf. Bea walked through the anti-theft gate, the heavy book held flat at stomach level.

The book fit perfectly over *La Vitesse*'s steering wheel. Bea read through the dragon entry twice to make sure she hadn't missed anything, but there wasn't much. European dragons were voracious. They slaughtered, consumed, and laid waste to the land until finally stopped by a great hero.

Bea had lived all her life in the bush, but she knew this much about the world: Heroes were more mythical than dragons. They simply didn't exist.

"Slow down, honey," Bea said. "Turn on Switzer."

La Vitesse shuddered. Rosie had the gas pedal flat on the floor. They'd be in the RCMP parking lot in minutes. But first, they had to take a sharp right onto Switzer Drive.

"I said slow down," Bea repeated.

Rosie didn't slow.

"What are you doing?" Bea screeched as they blew through the intersection.

"Do you want it to grab us again?" Rosie said.

Rosie flipped the latch on the driver's side window, stuck out her hand and pointed the mirror at the sky behind them. The dragon was still following, ten lengths behind and high above the highway.

"We've got lots of room," Bea pleaded. She gripped her daughter's shoulder and pointed at the last access point to the service road, coming up fast on their right. "Slow down and turn."

Rosie shrugged off her mother's hand. "Too late now."

Tears sprang to Bea's eyes. "Rosie, baby. You can't do this."

The rest of the highway was a straight shot through Edson and on to Edmonton. Three and a half hours of bush. But Hinton had service roads lining either side of the highway, busy with gas stations and strip malls. Not much traffic this early in the morning, but someone must have spotted the dragon by now. They were probably already running to a pay phone.

Bea raced to the back of the bus. The glass was clearer now, its coat of grime smeared thin by the dragon's swinging body. A little red Datsun chugged along in the right lane. Bea caught a glimpse of the driver's shocked expression, their mouth open in a perfect *O* as *La Vitesse* roared past.

High above the highway, the dragon folded its wings. It seemed to hover in the air. Then it dropped toward the tiny car like a torpedo.

It hit with all fours like a pouncing cat, talons puncturing the flimsy fibreglass roof. The car swerved through the median and plunged across the oncoming lanes. The dragon rode the car like a rodeo cowboy, legs flexing, wings slapping the air as if it could lift the car right off the road.

"Brake, brake," Bea whispered. "Throw it—Oh no."

Hinton's Husky station was the biggest in town, impossible to miss with the massive Canada flag snapping above. Big diesel pumps for the semis, four banks of regular pumps for the summer tourist traffic. And the Datsun was out of control. It missed the first pump but hit the second. The station went up with a *whump*.

Orange flames. Boiling smoke. And from the conflagration rose the dragon. Its wings fanned the flames with long, lazy beats.

"Go, Rosie!" Bea howled. Maybe they could get around the next curve before it spotted them. "Faster!"

Maybe the dragon would attack another car, blow up another station. Did she want that? No — it was horrible — but neither did she want the dragon on their tail again.

Then *La Vitesse*'s horn blasted. One long, insistent, unending bellow.

"No, Rose!" Bea screamed.

The dragon's wings hitched. It flipped and turned, graceful as a swallow, scales shedding streams of smoke. Its eyes gleamed, two chilly points, square and level.

Bea lived in the bush. She'd seen plenty of cougars, and she knew this: when a predator's eyes focus on you, two orbs in perfect alignment, you are meat, meat, and nothing but meat. Whether you live or die is no longer in your control. Your fate lives between the claws and teeth of another.

"Honey, why?" Bea moaned. But there was no answer, never any answer with Rosie. She did as she pleased.

From the time her daughter was born, Bea's one goal was to keep her at home for as long as possible. With a kid as strong-willed as Rosie, that meant giving in, always. It also meant feeding her well. Tasty food, and lots of it. Though tiny as a baby, Rosie had always been a good eater. She'd grown big and tall — nearly six feet and still growing — with broad shoulders and big hands and feet.

The food was an important strategy. Bea knew from experience that, aside from weekend bush parties, going for pizza or fries with friends was pretty much the only thing a Hinton teenager could do to beat the boredom. Bea had been caught in that trap herself.

At sixteen, instead of getting on the school bus for the long ride home, Bea would head to Gus's Pizza. Then, she'd wait outside the IGA grocery and try to catch a ride home with a neighbour. But that didn't always work, so she started hitch-hiking. The first two times were fine. The third time, her social studies teacher picked her up. For a half an hour, he'd lectured her about the dangers of hitchhiking, and then pulled over and slipped his hand into her jeans. That's how she got pregnant.

Bea didn't want that to happen to her girl. So if the poutine at the L&W was good, Bea's was better—the fries crispier, the cheese gooier, the gravy dark brown and chunky with lumps of salty hamburger. And that was just the start. Bea's nut-crusted elk roast was perfection and her open-fire flatbread with homemade jam beat any cake. So when Rosie got to that dangerous age, she never even thought about staying behind after school. Why would she hang out with kids she hated and eat substandard snacks when her mom's food was so good?

Rosie scared her teachers, but Bea didn't care. If her daughter sat in the back of every class and did the bare minimum of work to pass, that was fine with Bea. And if she stomped down the hallways with her elbows out, glaring at the other kids from under her ragged, dyed-black bangs and wore the same two Slayer T-shirts for a year, that was better than fine. Nobody would ever take advantage of her Rosie. Anyone who tried never tried twice.

La Vitesse **blasted east,** the speedometer topping out, the dragon still chasing them, and nothing ahead but open highway. Soon, they'd start climbing Obed Mountain. The engine couldn't take it at speed. Bea had to do something, but she was too scared to think. Scared of what the dragon would do when the bus began toiling up that long, steep slope. And also, for the first time in her life, she was scared of her daughter.

Rosie hunched in Bea's seat, her mouth set in a permanent sneer. The remnants of her blue-black lipstick smeared her chin. Maybe the biggest danger they faced wasn't the dragon. Maybe it was Rosie. Maybe it always had been.

The kids knew Rosie was dangerous. They'd always known. Bea made a habit of looking away when the kids scooted past Rosie's shotgun seat as if it were on fire. She ignored it when Rosie snarled at a tardy kid, and when she snagged a treat out of one of their backpacks, Bea treated it like a joke.

Bea knelt beside the driver's seat and put a gentle hand on her daughter's thick wrist.

"Honey, whatever I've done, I'm so sorry. But take it out on me, not the kids."

Rosie's brow furrowed. The bridge of her nose crinkled like she smelled something rotten.

"Don't talk shit, Mom," she snarled.

Bea moved her hand up to her daughter's bicep and tried again.

"You've been angry for a long time, haven't you? And now you're in control. And you do have control. You're making all the choices. So make the right one, honey. Turn us around."

"Fuck, Mom, what do you think I am?" Rosie said. She took a deep breath and screamed, "Hang on!"

Rosie slammed on the clutch and brakes and spun the wheel. The momentum threw Bea down the stepwell. She hit her head on the door, hard. By the time she'd shaken off the pain and climbed to her feet, *La Vitesse* sat idling in the middle of Pedley Road, a gravel-top dead-end with nothing along it but a few old houses tucked back deep in the bush.

"Good girl, thank you. I'll drive now." Bea laid a hand on her daughter's thick shoulder. It was solid as stone. Rosie's right hand strangled the steering wheel and her left stuck stiffly out the window, twisting the side-view mirror to scan the sky behind them.

"No," Rosie said quietly. "Stop touching me."

Rosie shifted the bus into first gear, then second. They rolled up the road. Over the soft crunch of wheels on gravel and the engine's low hum, the *whump-whump* of wide wings sounded, louder and louder. Behind Bea, the children sniffled and sobbed. Maybe Bea did too. She knew she should fight — but how? Bea had never hit anyone. Certainly not her child. Not ever. How could she have known it was a mistake?

"I'm sorry," Bea whispered. "I didn't know what I was doing. I was too young."

When Rosie answered, her voice was flat and emotionless. "Stop. I'm trying to think."

"I should have made you play with the other kids. I wanted to keep you home. Keep you safe. I didn't know what it would mean. That you'd be isolated. That it would be bad for you."

Bea leaned her left cheek against Rosie's arm as *La Vitesse* rolled toward the Pedley railway crossing. The lights flashed red under the white-and-black crossing sign. A train was coming, but Rosie was utterly focused on the side mirror, jaw clenched, eyes narrow.

The train's low horn sounded in the crossing pattern. Two short blasts, one long, one short. Bea put a soft hand on her daughter's fist where it gripped the wheel.

"We have to stop before the tracks, honey."

No answer. Bea climbed to her feet. The fire extinguisher lay in the aisle, beside a tiny sneaker that had slipped off the foot of a terrified child. A child who was in her care. A child she had to keep safe.

She hoisted the heavy extinguisher in her arms. Bea knew herself. Violence wasn't in her nature. She'd never raised a hand to anyone, even when she should have. Even when they were hurting her. Now she had to hurt her daughter. Had to. Lift the extinguisher high and drop it on Rosie's head. That's all.

But she couldn't. She put the extinguisher down and turned away.

The bus's front wheels bounced over the rails. The train raced toward them, a massive stack of silver metal topped by a curved glass windshield. Close now, so close Bea could see its wipers stuck at a low angle across the glass. Its horn screamed as it bore down on them with all its murderous weight and velocity. Rosie still had her hand out the side window, yanking at the mirror with her thick fingers.

Behind *La Vitesse*, at the bus's grimy rear window, a shadow reached out to wrap its wings around the bus. Then a wall of silver speed obliterated it.

Rosie couldn't get the bus door open. Not even with both hands and all her muscle and weight.

"Mom, how the fuck do you do this?"

"There's a trick to it." Bea slipped her soft hands over her daughter's and flicked the rubber thumb control on *La Vitesse*'s spring-latched handle. She cranked the door open, just as she'd done a thousand times before, but never with such relief.

The train was still rolling past, brakes howling and throwing sparks. When it had cleared the crossing, Bea ushered the kids off the bus.

"You too," she told Rosie, and followed her daughter down to solid ground.

Bea wrapped her sweater around little Michelle Arsenault and lifted her up to settle on her hip. She wiped the child's nose with a crumpled tissue from her jeans pocket, then lifted Tony Lalonde onto her other hip.

At the railroad crossing, the tar-smeared sleepers and silver rails were painted with red-brown gore, thick and smoking. The dragon's head lay beside *La Vitesse*'s right rear wheel. Bleeding pits marked the milky sclera of its eyes, and a blue liquid leaked from its fanged jaws.

Rosie heaved the dragon's head so it lay chin-down on the road.

"Where's the rest of it?" Michelle Lalonde whispered from under Bea's elbow.

"Here, in the ditch," Rosie said. She slipped down the icy incline and hefted a tattered wing, then dragged it up to the road and deposited it beside the dragon's head.

"That's not good meat," said Blair Tocher, eleven years old and an experienced hunter. "Smells like bear gone bad. You can't eat that."

"I think Rosie could," Joan Cardinal said.

Bea shivered, cold without her sweater, and her forearm was wet where she was supporting little Tony Lalonde against her body. His arms gripped Bea's neck and his little snot-smeared face burrowed into her.

"Is someone coming to help us?" he asked in a whisper.

"Soon, I think."

Far up the tracks, the train had finally stopped. The engineer would have already reported the incident. She couldn't hear the sirens yet, but it wouldn't be long.

Rosie dragged the dragon's torso from the far side of the tracks. Its gut had split open, revealing a nest of mottled entrails padded with honeycombed tissue.

"The dragon you saw on Roche Miette was red, Mom." Rosie stripped off her gore-soaked gloves and dropped them on the ground. "That's what you said."

"That's right," said Bea. "And you didn't believe me."

"Then this isn't the only dragon." Rosie shaded her eyes with her hand and scanned the sky.

Bea nodded. "There must be one more at least."

Tony whimpered. Bea hitched him up higher on her hip.

"We're okay. We're safe," she told the kids. "Right, Rose?"

Rosie shrugged and drew a pack of menthols from her pocket. A cigarette dangled from her lips as she fished for her lighter. She glanced at Bea, furtively, as if she needed her mother's permission to light up in front of the kids. Bea almost laughed.

She'd thought there were no heroes, but she was wrong. Dead wrong.

"Go ahead and smoke, honey," Bea said. "You earned it."

FEATURE INTERVIEW

Kelly Robson

Pulp Literature: *'La Vitesse' takes us back to the early 1980s in the foothills of Alberta. What inspired you to write about mothers, daughters, and dragons in that setting?*

Kelly Robson: I come from a place that doesn't get written about, so I've been trying for years to rectify that. But there's a problem. While some writers are really good at illustrating the place and time where they grew up, I'm not. I'd been struggling and failing to write stories set in Hinton for years. Maybe my failure was because my feelings about the place are so ambivalent, so complex. It's a beautiful place, but also ugly in every way. Its history is fascinating, but also brutal. In any case, this story was my first breakthrough at approaching it. To succeed, I had to posit a story with a very concrete problem and a lot of action. The emotional content comes around the edges.

PL: *It's refreshing to see a mother as the main character of a genre story. Although Bea suggests Rosie is the hero of the story, it takes a hero to raise a hero. Can you tell us more about Bea and Rosie, and why you wanted to write about them?*

KR: My sister drives a school bus in Hinton, so I know the stories, and I know a school bus driver carries a lot of responsibility for other people's kids. I also thought it was important to make Bea a Métis woman, like Mrs Oulette, the school bus driver of my youth. Bea and Rosie live on the lands of their people. Since childhood, it's seemed to me a terrible injustice that the Indigenous people of Jasper and Banff National Parks were all kicked out of their ancestral lands when the parks were formed. (I can't help but note here it didn't happen to the white people who had cottages in Thousand Islands National Park, formed around the same time). So I present Bea and Rosie as survivors, who belong on the land of my childhood in a way I never did, and whose descendants will continue to thrive there in the future.

Which brings up a question: Is a white person allowed to write about Indigenous people? I think so, as long as it's done in an honest and non-fetishizing way, and for reasons that are inherent to the story. I feel like that's the case here. If I'd made Bea and Rosie into Anglo characters, it would erase the Indigenous population of the area and play into a white saviour narrative instead.

PL: *In 2017, you were a finalist for the Astounding Award for Best New Writer and won the Nebula for your story* A Human Stain. *How did this recognition impact your writing career? What advice do you have for emerging writers striving to make their mark in the speculative fiction genre?*

KR: New writers should lean into what makes them unique—their individual cultural and social perspectives, their own personal ways of seeing the world, their focus on the types of stories that are important to them. Editors want this! But also at the same time, fiction is a seduction, you have to find ways to lure readers into your narrative, make them care about your point of view. So, it's a balancing act. How can you tell a story that is both completely unique and undeniably magnetic? The answer is, be yourself, but a version of yourself that is an excellent storyteller. That takes dedication and practice. Never stop working at it.

PL: *As someone who has explored a variety of genres, do you find any common threads or themes that consistently emerge in your writing, regardless of the genre?*

KR: I'm constantly writing about parenthood, but not in the usual way. Many of my characters choose to be caregivers and mentors. Even here in 'La Vitesse', Bea isn't just Rosie's mom; she also cares for and protects the kids on her bus route. She's a nurturer. Her responsibility doesn't end with her own kid but extends far into her community. Even when I think I'm writing a story that doesn't touch on caregiving, it usually ends up having that element. I can't get away from it. I think the reason is (and I say this as a childless person) it's the most important and most difficult thing in the world, and inherently hopeful.

PL: *How do you continue to experiment with and evolve in your craft?*

KR: Reading. Reading is always the most important thing a writer can do to benefit their own work. I read widely, in all genres along with lots of nonfiction. I work at staying intellectually curious. I have a long list of stories I'd like to try to write, and some of them I'm not ready for —I don't have the skills to pull them off, yet. More reading and writing is required!

PL: *Thank you so much for this. Before we let you go, tell us: what are you working on now?*

KR: Yet again, I'm trying to figure out how to write a full-length novel. I'm currently at the stage where I'm wondering if I just can't really work at that length. But I've been through a lot of emotional turmoil lately, so maybe I just have to lean in and trust the process. That's the advice I'd give someone else in this situation, certainly.

PL: *Whatever you come up with, and whatever the length, we can't wait to read more wonderful, nurturing, Kelly Robson fiction!*

THE 2023 KINGFISHER POETRY PRIZE

THE 2023 KINGFISHER POETRY PRIZE

In honour of Pulp Literature's tenth anniversary, we introduced a new contest for short poems: the Kingfisher Poetry Prize. Poets from far and wide answered our call, and we received an outstanding selection of works. With the help of our talented judges, first reader Emily Osborne and final judge Jude Neale, we are pleased to have narrowed down the entrants to crown our winning Kingfisher and select two honourable mentions. Here they are, with Jude's comments.

Winner: 'Most of Your Stuff is Worthless' by Leanne Boschman

This poem speaks of weight and weightlessness that we live with. … A truly enchanting poem, always moving the reader along toward a surprising ending with a delicate twist.

Honourable Mention: 'The Dahlia Truth' by Pattie Palmer-Baker

This fresh and blooming poem can almost be read from end to beginning! It is dredged in colour and form.

Honourable Mention: 'Kid Gloves' by Marri Champié

This poem speaks deftly and matter-of-factly of the ageing process, particularly of the hands. But also of so much more.

And congratulations to the poets who made the 2023 Kingfisher shortlist:

Angela Rebrec for 'Behold, I have inscribed you on the palm of my hand'
Callista Markotich for 'Mother and Son'
Cara Waterfall for 'sel·vage'
Chelsea Comeau for 'Somass Estuary, Late Summer'
Dean Gessie for 'gastropod'
Diana Hayes for 'Postcards from Sitka'
Jade Y Liu for '怀念' ('In Memory')
Leah Hart for 'Phoenix'
Leanne Boschman for 'Most of Your Stuff is Worthless'
Marri Champié for 'Kid Gloves'
Pattie Palmer-Baker for 'The Dahlia Truth'
Veronika Gorlova for 'Water Restrictions'

Leanne Boschman has loved the music and mystery of poetry for her entire life. Her work has appeared in journals and anthologies, and her first collection, Precipitous Signs: A Rain Journal, was published in 2009. Leanne's second collection of poems, Here at the Crux, came out in 2022. She has taught academic writing and literature in post-secondary institutions for over thirty years. Leanne participates in several writing groups and poetry reading series and is passionate about community development through the arts.

Most of Your Stuff is Worthless

by Leanne Boschman

Hutch, armoire, credenza — our offspring do not want
these heavy relics, belongings that have laid such claim on us.
When asked by grandchildren about my youthful chores I recount
how weekly with lemon oil I anointed each hulking fixture,
my parents' old bedroom suite in my room when they upgraded.
Later the nicked desks, faded dining room tables of our student days
ferreted away from second-hand furniture shops —
those mausoleums of what were once teeming woodlands.

After her parents died, my friend from Belgium shipped at great cost
imposing cabinets, bed-frames, tapestries — how they filled
her farmhouse on Vancouver Island, her loyalty to them even after
her childhood where everything was ancient grudges, incursions,
stone-coldness.

Grandson, what will you have to pay for our possessions?
You who only five years ago took up a small space, the translucent
membrane of your skin, small buds of your fingers lengthening.
You were born in a city that was once coastal rainforest,
where our affection filled the room where you arrived, flourished
before we had given you even the weight
of a name.

Title quotation from blog written by Sibhan Kratovil, Estate Planning Lawyer

Pattie Palmer-Baker lives in Portland, Oregon, with her beloved husband. Over the years of exhibiting her artwork——paste-paper collages with poetry in calligraphic form——she was surprised and delighted to discover that people do indeed like poetry. She now concentrates on writing. Pattie has won several first prizes and has been nominated twice for the Pushcart Poetry Prize. Published in many journals, she is also the author of the chapbook The Color of Goodbye *and the poetry collection* Five Fundamental Forces.

THE DAHLIA TRUTH

BY PATTIE PALMER-BAKER

Oh those dahlias!
A drill sergeant's dream of puffball perfection,
they fold out in lemony layers,
salute orange, stand straight,
face the sun, size to coffee cups,
and line up in a platoon of primary colors.

I cannot resist all this symmetry.
I push through the inch-wide rows,
palpate their raspberry-red flesh,
touch their purple pulse.

Just beyond the reach of my eyelash
looms an argiope spider bigger

than the eye of my center, shredding
any Van Gogh colour-soaked reverie.

You need to know say the dahlias finger caresses
and moony eyes are nothing to us.
The spider nestles in the cups of our petals,
we lick the silk from their spindled legs.

Three-time Dell Award-winning author **Marri Champié** *has often ridden horse-back into the Sawtooth Wilderness. Marri was nominated for a Pushcart Prize for poetry in 2015. In 2013 she received the Boise State University President's Writing Award for fiction and poetry, and in 2018 won an Oregon Poetry Association Award. Her novel,* Silverhorn, *appeared in 2018, and the sequel,* Firemoon, *will be released later this year. Marri works as a wildland fire-support driver and lives on a small ranch overlooking the Idaho prairie.*

Kid Gloves

by Marri Champié

Like my mother now, my hands are frail, sun-spotted.
Are these blue veins just map cords of the road traveled?
Once calloused, unyielding, these tools are now knotted;
I'm memory-struck by a life story unravelled.
Helitack guy, lightning-bolt smile, ember-lit eyes.
He takes my hand, runs his thumb across the hard palm
Do I not wear gloves to work? he asks, and dives
into his pack. Fire gloves, resistant to napalm,
to identify pilots even if they burn.
I told my mother I'd wear those gloves all the time
so my hands wouldn't look old or weathered, or turn
ancient. Despite the years, my palms are smooth and fine.
It was helitack guy with the kid gloves who lied.
I handled him gently but it was suicide.

TAKE MY HAND: A GHOST STORY

Mel Anastasiou

Mel Anastasiou *writes the Fairmount Manor Mysteries, the Hert-fordshire Pub Mysteries, and the Monument Studios Mysteries. Winner of a Literary Titan Gold award and longlisted for the Leacock Medal, Mel is also the author of two illustrated thirty-day workbooks on story structure: the steampunk-themed* The Writer's Boon Companion *and* The Writer's Friend and Confidante. *For news on published and upcoming new works, visit her website, melanastasiou.wordpress.com.*

Mel's latest paranormal mystery begins early in the 9 0s, in the night-time wards of a city hospital, with a young orderly in hiding.

©2024, Mel Anastasiou

Take My Hand
Part 1: Off to Never-Never Land

Chapter 1
April 1991

Jamie Stewart was a creature of the night, by choice and by necessity. Because she always took night-shift work, she would have been popular with the daytime orderlies if they'd ever laid their well-rested eyes on her. Jamie avoided the day shift of her own free will. She wouldn't have taken it if she were asked.

It was Jamie's opinion that the phrase *you can run but you can't hide* was untrue, or at least that it ought to be amended to *you can't hide for long.* In the short term, these dim corridors, darkened patient rooms, and unoccupied waiting areas remained places of safety for her as much as for the patients. For one thing, the hospital was badly lit, and, like vampires and nocturnal rodents, she didn't consider shadows to be eerie. Darkness protected her from discovery.

Some nights a patient woke up and cried out. It was Jamie's job and her privilege to make them comfortable and help them back to sleep if she could. To this end she talked to wakeful patients about what awaited them when they returned to the world outside, which was to say she made up stories out of her imagination because she had so little experience of the world, especially in the sunlit hours.

Tonight, she set her bucket and mop aside in order to spend fifteen minutes with a woman undergoing much testing. Maria pronounced herself aghast that Jamie had never played cribbage. She pulled her crib board, matchsticks, and playing cards out of her alligator handbag. Two losing games later, Jamie left to mop the central corridor.

She said, "Thanks for teaching me how to play."

Maria called after her, "But I didn't teach you how to win," and dealt herself solitaire.

Amazing, how little preparation one needed for the job of keeping people clean, comfortable, and, if possible, alive. Orderlies learned on the job; they learned quickly or got out. The work, even the mopping, made Jamie as happy as she'd ever been, and she cautioned herself not to grow too attached to the hospital or the patients. When she left, it would be the same as the last time and the time before: her belongings in a duffel bag and a dash into darkness. The follow-up call to her supervisor from a phone box at the bus station would consist of a lie to excuse her swift departure, and the truth of her gratitude for the job she'd hate to leave.

Jamie sluiced out her bucket and poured the black water down the custodial closet drain. She refilled her pail and mopped along the shadows and out into the half-light.

Like every other shift on the wards, there was always something new to learn. She improved her understanding of cleaning methods, of course. Further, she gained new perspectives on living by chatting with her patients, especially the elderly ones. Ailing and declining, they were still far more knowledgeable than she could dream of being. They had much to tell her regarding foreign travel in the days of their prosperous middle age and various clever ways they'd hoodwinked poverty when they were young. She absorbed some kind of new understanding from every one of them, even the ones who never said a word. For example, the elderly woman who'd died on Tuesday without regaining consciousness had taught her that a person has time to think about someone or something they love before dying with a smile. That smile turned Jamie's heart upside down. She'd held the old woman's lifeless hand until the family arrived.

Privately Jamie divided the patients in her wing into two groups. First were the short-term patients. These came and went, like fellow travellers on parallel paths whose routes diverged when they returned to life or, like the woman who smiled, departed this world altogether.

The second, much smaller set was comprised of a handful of indefinite stay patients: people in the coma ward. She left her chores in this ward until last, generally around three o'clock in the morning. Unless there was some pressing need in emergency, she spent extra time in the coma ward. She'd noticed that this was the area most likely to be spit-and-promised by the day orderlies. It was an understandable oversight given the pressures and difficulties daytime work brought. But in the dark of night, Jamie was most often free to take her time and clean undisturbed. She scoured deeply into corners and along angles where walls met floors and employed the duster with tender caution inside the grille-work on various machines. She talked to the patients all the while.

Once, a night nurse had caught her talking to them, and, far from disapproving, told Jamie that one never knew what might help unconscious patients. Emboldened, she discovered she enjoyed these one-sided conversations, as it was the only time she could speak freely without fear of revealing her origins to anyone who might speak of them: of her escape from captivity, or the careful balancing act that was her present situation.

She mopped through the doors into the coma ward and the private rooms for those who could pay for them. She wiped down the skirting boards and finished at the bedside of one of the oldest and longest-term patients. She took his hand in hers.

The week before, she was certain his fingers had moved. When she let the night nurse know, the nurse shook her head but suggested Jamie press the call button by the old man's bedside if he squeezed her hand or gave any sign of consciousness.

"Coma patients do come around sometimes," the nurse said. There was nothing encouraging in her tone. "Which one is he?"

Jamie almost gave the bed number, but stopped herself and called him by the name on the chart clipped to the foot of his bed. "His name is G Gordon."

"G for …?"

"The chart doesn't say."

"Well, you keep an eye on him, that's all. But we won't hold our breath."

"I'll watch him," Jamie said. "I'll tell you if he wakes."

"You do that very thing," the nurse said. "I know you're not the kind to get behind on your work. And G Gordon could sure use a visitor."

Sitting with G Gordon was not a chore. Jamie learned as much from the coma patients as she did from the wakeful ones. Until she'd spent time among them, she thought she knew everything about keeping the lowest of profiles. For example, she used a name that was not easily traced, since *Jamie* could be a man or a woman. And *Stewart* was a fairly common name, but not ostentatiously so, like *Smith.* She worked at night, blacked out her small apartment windows with tinfoil, and never answered her door. But these precautions hadn't prevented the envelope finding its way under her previous apartment door six months before, and on the other side of the continent. It would find her again. But not yet. Not tonight.

Tonight, G Gordon's dry hand was motionless in hers. His papery eyelids and waxen skin hadn't changed since yesterday, either for better or worse. His sunken chest rose and fell in shallow breaths. Where there was life, there was hope of awakening.

But somewhere between one and two in the morning, his breathing grew noisier. The rales rang so loudly in the quiet ward that for a moment she imagined every coma patient would sit up and open bright wet stares in her direction. But that was foolishness at a cinematic level, and she cursed herself for disengaging her attention from G Gordon. With her free hand, she pushed the call button for the night nurse. As it turned out, it was lucky she calmed down and stayed with him, because with one last rattling breath, he died. She sat beside his bed, still holding his hand.

When a patient died, it was Jamie's practice to murmur some personal tribute to mark the moment of the patient's passing. Her words were often inspired by visitors, get-well cards, or snapshots on the bedside stands. She might say, *Your grandchildren will remember how you sat with them beside the lake and floated daisy chains on the water.* Or, *Won't your son be proud of the deck you built for him; he'll never forget it was you who hammered the boards holding up his barbecue.* However, G Gordon hadn't any visitors, cards, or photos, and Jamie knew nothing beyond what she'd observed of his sleeping features. But she liked him anyway, and that was enough.

She folded both her hands around his and spoke quietly. "I'm sorry you didn't wake up after all. But I want to say that I learned quite a lot from you, G Gordon, about how to be invisible in plain view. I don't know whether you ever had to hide from anybody, but I do, and it's helpful to see that when you don't look at other people, they don't look back at you. Someday, when I'm in a tight spot, I'll use that method successfully, and I'll have you to thank for my safety. I'll call it the G Gordon Method for turning invisible. And because of your method, I won't forget you."

The nurse arrived, closely followed by a doctor. Jamie covered G Gordon and took him on a gurney down to the morgue. When she returned, she stripped the empty bed and wiped down the furniture. Next, she took a cloth and applied elbow grease to the window ledges and mouldings, which took her into the darkest areas of the wards and the ends of corridors. Here, equipment trolleys made oddly shaped shadows, and a more skittish person than Jamie might have glanced over her shoulder now and then. But so long as she was free, shadows had no power to frighten her.

So it was that Jamie had no warning. She sensed no subsonic rumblings in the corridor. The bed curtains didn't ripple with the passage of something she'd rather not see. The sleepers in the rooms around her could have muttered and sobbed at a sudden shared dream, but they did not.

All was calm.

And then an unseen hand covered Jamie's. The hair rose on the back of her neck, and she sat down hard at a nurse's desk.

She clasped her left hand over her right and held it tight against the desktop.

Without violence, but with great strength, the invisible hand unlaced her fingers and forced her to take hold of the stack of computer printouts on the desk. She tried to resist, or maybe it was more accurate to say that she tried to try, but she found herself flipping the first bundle of paper over so the blank sides of the pages faced upwards.

Jamie watched her hand move as if it weren't part of her at all, as if it were a great fleshy tarantula and she couldn't be sure where it would drop next. It groped at the desktop, found a ballpoint, and scratched with it at the slab of paper.

The pen was upside down.

With a movement of irritation her hand snapped the pen down onto the desk and took up the correct end.

Jamie watched as her hand wrote a message on the paper:

I DO NOT

The writing was round and a little old-fashioned looking, unlike her own jagged handwriting. The pen trailed off the paper and seemed about to scrawl across the metal surface of the desk. Jamie ripped the top page aside, and her hand moved over to begin again.

I DON'T KNOW WHO I AM.

"Stop," Jamie whispered. The word tasted weak in her mouth, and she stirred herself to fight back. She would use both hands to pull out of the invisible grip. This ought to have been an easy win, two flesh-and-bone hands against one unseen hand-shaped force. But no matter how fiercely she pushed and pulled against it, the invisible hand held tight.

In the end, she gave into it and let go, somewhat the way G Gordon had let go of life. She lost all consciousness of the ward around her. Thereafter, in that round, clear hand, with sudden stops and starts, the spirit told his story through the small hours of the night.

Chapter 2

I don't know who I am, and I have no idea how far I have wandered or where I have landed. At first I'm so dazed that I don't care, but then I look down.

I can't see my hands.

This makes me mad, and like a spanked new-born I ride into the world on a grudge, demanding my rights. My right hand. Also my left. And, for Pete's sake, the rest of me.

It occurs to me that if I'm going to have a body, I'd better have some context to put it in. Most people take time and space for granted, but then most people can see their hands.

I look on time and space.

Or, since it seems I can't even count on having eyes, possibly I perceive.

Compared with my physical situation, this room feels comfortingly ordinary. The clubfoot bed and squat bureau have no power to surprise me, and although I can't remember this particular room, it seems inevitable that the ceiling hunches down around the gabled window above a shabby padded seat. If I had hands, I could give the cushion a punch and I know that dust would puff out of it like warm breath on a cold morning.

There's a door by the bed. Not the door that I'm afraid of.

And there's somebody on the bed.

A blue light from a box on a low table lights the face of the adolescent boy on the bed. He's dressed all in black, top to toe. His sock feet rest on the headboard, and he's facing the bed's foot, gazing into the glowing box. He looks unreal, with perfect white skin and dark-drawn brows, like a vampire.

Like a ghost.

I can't see my feet, but I determine to move across the room towards him. I do this by remembering how a fish moves, and I work up a nice little ripple that takes me towards the bed. I'm careful not to let the transparent piece of space and time that is me touch the wall on the way. I don't want to know whether I'd ripple right through it and out into the night.

I reach the bed.

"Are you real?" I ask the boy, because by now I have the feeling that someone in this room isn't entirely human, and I'm hoping it's him.

The boy stirs and looks at the door, or at his reflection in the mirror on the door. He doesn't answer or look at me, although I'm standing close enough to him to raise the hairs on the back of his neck with my breath. But I don't seem to be breathing.

From inside the box, something roars, and somebody screams like a siren. The shock of it lifts me a couple of feet into the air. I hang there, kicking helplessly at nothing, like a cat dancing by its scruff.

I calm down by concentrating on my rippling movement. I copy the boy's position so that I'm floating a flat twenty-five inches above the ground.

Together we stare at the box on the table. I whisper, "Gosh."

The box we're staring at looks a lot like a radio because of its size and shape. Actually, it's more like something out of *Amazing*

Science Fiction Stories, because there's a moving picture right in the box. I see a monster ape stomping atop a building like it was on fire, and the screaming is coming from the girl the ape is holding in his hand.

I know this movie. It's *King Kong.*

When I saw *King Kong* a couple of years ago, I sat right up in the front row with my brother Ted, our eyes bulging and focusing in the dark, so close you'd swear Kong's breath smelled like popcorn. After it was over, we tumbled out of the movie house, blinking in the sunlight under the marquee. The moviegoers streaming past us looked, after Kong, like tiny fine-featured elves.

Kong scared the daylights out of Ted and me, but in the little box he looks like a wind-up toy, and the young fellow next to me yawns and blinks. Although I'm not tired, somehow I know it's very late at night.

I recognize the box with moving pictures now. I read about it in a newspaper report on the World's Fair. Not long ago, I think it must have been the summer of 1936, I read about the scientific exhibits there in *Life* magazine, and there were pictures, too. There was a cat that had been frozen and then revived, although no one was certain whether the process had slowed its reflexes or if it had been clumsy to start with. And there was a box like this one. It was called television. The screen was a lot smaller and fuzzier than this. At the time I thought the cat was more interesting.

On the television screen, Kong disappears. The film reel has snapped, I think, and I wait for the boy to open the back of the television to fix it. Will he use celluloid tape to stick the ends of the film strip together? I have seen this before at the movies, and I remember how we all stamped and whistled in the dark, and how the lemon drops crunched like bones under our feet.

Now—and I'm certain this was not in *King Kong*—I see a coloured scene of a hundred Flash Gordon cars and a man in a cowboy hat who is hitting the cars with a baseball bat. After this he seems to want somebody to buy them. I'm beginning to think time and space aren't all they're cracked up to be when the film splits and I see a plate of doughnuts iced with pink sugar. They look almost real, and without thinking I reach out to touch them.

I see my hand.

I yell like Kong.

This time I go all the way up to the ceiling, and my companion sits up straight and looks around.

"Did you see that?" I shout. He scowls and turns back to the television.

I move downwards quite capably now. When I reach the foot of the bed, I slowly extend what I believe to be my right hand into the wash of the television light. My fingertips appear first, then knuckles, and on down to my palm and wrist.

My good old hand.

I push my left hand into the light, and as I look closer I see that it's not actually the light that is causing my hand to be visible. It's the dust particles in the air, glowing as they reflect the light from minute surfaces that give me shape. My hands don't look like flesh. I seem to be wearing skin-tight wrist-length gloves of some glowing material.

Turning in triumph, I see that my companion is on his feet. His eyes are round. And despite the fact that King Kong is back on the screen, I think it's probably my disembodied hands floating at the foot of his bed that have scared him upright.

"Well, what do you know?" I say.

Oh, I can't help myself. I wave at him.

And he's gone. Out the door. I want to call after him, to apologize, but I don't know his name, and anyway I'm laughing too hard.

Never mind.

I'd hold my breath if I were breathing, but as it is I move my head up into the illuminated dust. I remember the mirrored door and turn to look.

There I am.

I'm the head and neck of a young man, around twenty years old, whose hair needs brushing. I stop short at the round collar of my shirt. My eyes blink, and my head turns. My head looks like a large version of a blown glass ball flecked with gold and silver, the kind of thing you float in a fishpond.

I smile, and my teeth glisten unearthly white.

My image angles away from me. The bedroom door is opening.

The young fellow in black sits himself down with his back against the headboard of his bed. My head floats on a level with his. He looks right at me, possibly a little bit through me, and tells me that his name is Dylan. Being addressed as a thinking being this way makes me so happy that I almost miss his words.

"Can I ask, how are you creating sound? I'll bet it feels like your neck is vibrating."

"Like your hand is shaking, for example?" I ask.

He covers one hand with the other and holds it still. "I'm not as frightened as I should be."

"Me neither." I say. "And it's not my neck that's vibrating. It's more like I'm using the whole room as a sound box, I guess."

"Like a guitar?"

"Or a ukulele."

"But your voice comes out of your mouth."

"Just like yours. Wonders never cease, do they?"

We study one another, face to face. And, really, face is about all there is to me. I don't want to move out of the dusty light that gives me shape. Although I stop at my collar, well above my torso, I find that when I move my mouth and my eyes I feel almost like myself. Like a real person. I blink, therefore I am.

"I have another question," Dylan says.

"I hope it's got less science in it than the last one."

But Dylan only wants to know what to call me.

"Easy. Okay." I nod. "I am ..."

I pause. This isn't such an easy question after all. I seem to have a blank where my name should be. It's like when you're dreaming and you find you've forgotten your street number, or your clothes, and if you could just remember one important fact you would be home and warm.

I know I have a name. It's not a difficult name. I can't imagine how I could have forgotten it. I reach into memory and for a moment I think I've got it, but it turns into a memory I'm trying to escape. The door, looming dark and close. On the other side of the door is something I don't want to see.

I push away from it, and in memory I hear my brother Ted say my name.

Casee.

Casey.

I like the taste of my name when I say it aloud.

The satisfaction of knowing my name helps to fill the emptiness underneath my collar. I raise my hand into the light to shake his, but he eyes me sideways.

He says, "Maybe I should say, *Greetings.*"

"It's not Christmas. Is it?"

"Aliens say *greetings*," he says with a straight face. He holds out his hand. "Have you come from outer space?"

I might have known: when we try to shake, his hand passes through my fingers. Dylan pulls back his hand and looks at it, but it's not even dusty.

"You think I'm a spaceman?" In the mirror I watch my mouth make the words. For the first time I can smell the dust in the air. Suddenly the room feels old. And cold.

"*Take me to your leader.*" His eyes widen with mischief. If he is right, I hope for his sake that I'm a friendly alien, one who doesn't mind being joshed.

When I don't smile, Dylan clears his throat. He adds, "Oh, well, leader, follower, all I follow are soap operas."

Of course, his silliness may spring from nerves.

If I were an alien, would I know about soap operas? Would I remember a mother who warmed up the radio with half an hour to spare? She buttered sandwiches for my father's lunchbox while she listened to *Just Plain Bill* and *The Guiding Light*. At dinner she'd bring Ted and my dad and me up to date on the soap opera characters' lives like they were distant relations.

I say with confidence, "I'm not a spaceman."

He screws up his face. "I was hoping for a scientific explanation. But let's move on to magic. Are you a genie?"

His eyes take on a calculating look, and I can tell he is marshalling wishes.

I look at the bottles on the floor by the bed. Their shape is oddly bulbous, but I know their names. Pepsi-Cola, Coca-Cola. Aladdin's genie came out of a lamp. Could I have come out of a Pepsi-Cola bottle?

"I'm not a genie." There's another television screen on a bureau near his bed. Something blips back and forth without stopping. I become conscious of a sound like the squeak of a rubber ball bouncing.

I ask, "What's that?"

He glances over his shoulder. "*Power Mate Gold Leader Nine Thousand.*" He makes a face that says I ought to know what it is. His eyes narrow again. "It's a computer game. Are you sure you're not an alien?"

"Yes." I remind myself that I'm a guest in his room, uninvited if welcome, because I'm beginning to feel impatient with his sense of humour.

Dylan rolls onto his back and stretches arms and legs towards the ceiling. He rests in this position, like a sleeping dog in a matinee cartoon. Against his thin wrist I see the glowing face of his watch.

I point out the time. "It's three o'clock in the morning. Why are you awake at this hour?"

He rolls over to face me again. "I don't sleep at night. I do my sleeping in the day."

"What about school?"

"I sleep in school. It saves time. Watch." Dylan scrambles across the bed and kneels up to play his electric computer game. As he manipulates the steering stick, his expression tells me nothing of how the game is going. On the screen, however, a squat figure annihilates cavemen, knights in armour, and monsters from outer space.

Glad I am at least not a monster from outer space, I congratulate Dylan on his victory, and he shrugs at the screen.

"I practise all the time," he tells me. "Hey, you could be a time traveller. That would be a scientific explanation."

I see that he is being polite now.

We both know what I am.

"No." My sigh doesn't swirl the dust in the beam of light from the silent television. "It's 1937, home sweet home."

"It's not." Dylan names a date that's ridiculously different, more than fifty years later in fact. Most *Amazing Stories* don't take place this far into the future.

But he's the solid one. I have to believe him. I nearly choke on the word, but I manage to say, "Right. I see. It's 1991."

"So you might be a time traveller." He is trying to cheer me up.

We stare at each other.

I remember my Aunt Peggy, and her eyes as she counted up the sad few visitors to her sitting room in her last few months of life. She told my mother, "It's as if people thought dying was contagious." If she thought dying was lonely, what about being dead?

"I'm …"

We say it together.

"… a ghost."

Dylan's face is pale, perhaps slightly more than before. Nevertheless, his gaze is bright with interest.

"And you're haunting my house."

I almost answer, *It's not your house that's the issue. Anywhere I am, that's what I'll be doing. By definition, I'll be haunting.* But it would be churlish to say so, and my presence here isn't Dylan's fault.

He adds, "Why are you haunting my room?"

At this moment I don't care why. For the pressing question is, where have I been for half a century?

Here I am with no solid body and no clear answers.

Books are correct. Even more surprisingly, the moving pictures have it right. Death just isn't fair.

Dylan is acting the schoolboy, playing around with a lamp and one of the cushions from the window seat in an attempt to raise clouds of dust to make me visible when I move around his attic room. I can't seem to get a kick out of his dramatics. In fact I feel every one of my twenty years as I struggle to make sense of the passage of time and put my missing fifty years into perspective. 1991 isn't a date to me; it's only a number, too small to represent the number of books in a library, too large to represent the lined-up buns and cakes behind a bake shop window.

I escape into a corner of Dylan's bedroom, out of range of his experiments with small dust storms and directed light beams, and make a stab at assimilating the idea of so many years passing. Fifty Christmases, and no eggnog. Fifty birthdays, and no candles. Or wrinkles, apparently. Furthermore, when I seize my chance to think, it turns out that, like language, basic mathematics hasn't left me, or possibly has returned. I add the half century that has passed since my death to my grandfather's age at the time. The answer makes me blink. A subsequent sum, adding fifty to my parents' age, is equally discouraging. All three of them must be dead by now. The multiple loss stuns me. But couldn't my family be ghosts like me, haunting somebody's house? I wish it were this house. I picture the expression on my grandfather's face if he were to appear in Dylan's room, in a similar condition to my own. I'd bet a silver dollar Grandpop would be as baffled as I am by the situation, but his company would be welcome. So would my parents'. They were pretty good parents, old-fashioned of course, but they both laughed easily at any ragged old joke with which my brother Ted or I regaled them, the funny lines nicked from Fred Allen. *In our family tree, who's the sap? How do they get cows to sit down on the evaporated milk cans?* I wonder how my parents' lives turned out after my death. I worry that they broke their hearts on my early demise. Ted would have helped them get through it.

If it's 1991, It's possible my classmates at junior college are still around, and then of course Ted might be among the living as well, silver-haired and as soigné at seventy as he was at sixteen. In 1937, Ted was Dylan's age, as a matter of fact. I return my attention to Dylan, who's directing my movements with hand signals and barked commands, apparently oblivious of my actual position in his room and my lack of cooperation. I take pity on the lad and step into his illuminated cloud of cushion dust.

He says, "Casey, get with the program. Aren't you sick of standing around like a department store dummy? Fly upwards." Dylan aims the desk lamp at the ceiling like a ray gun.

"Lucky for you I'm a good sport. Like this?"

"Rad. Now, hover." He sits back with satisfaction. "This is how Spielberg must feel directing a King movie."

I hover. "*King Kong?*"

"Stephen King," he corrects me. And straightens me out. Apparently, the writer rules a dark literary country, and Princess Elizabeth is Queen of England now. This is confusing because she's still a little girl, ten years younger than I am.

Was.

Am. But it's not 1937 anymore.

"I've had sufficient," I tell Dylan. "Floating to the ceiling and looking down at the top of your head isn't as gripping an entertainment as you might think."

"How can you already be bored with being a ghost?"

"I admit that it's better with you here, despite your light-bulb shenanigans. But I hate the way floating reminds me of looking down at something that scares the heck out of me."

"Probably you had an out-of-body experience when you died," he says, as one might say *probably you had chicken pox.* "I've seen it all the time in ghost movies. You hang above your own body while they try to start up your heart again. Then either you come back to life …"

"… or you don't." I shake my head and move down to the bed to face him. I sit cross-legged like he does. Dylan hangs the desk lamp by its neck over the head of the bed so that the angled light outlines my whole body, give or take a knee and an elbow.

I say, "Forget the floating tricks. What do you think I'm doing here?"

I look him hard in the eye. With all his reading of ghost stories and fifty years more than me of scary movies, maybe he knows something I don't. He has that kind of secretive look about him.

Ted used to drive me crazy when he got secretive. A younger brother is supposed to be shorter and have less than a full tank when it comes to worldly experience. But Ted? He'd grin and hint at some hidden knowledge, like the import of our dad's most recent remark about us setting up our own radio to bring in our music shows. We admire Bing Crosby. *Nonsense crooning,* our father said. He refused to call popular songs real music. Ted might tell me, *I asked Dad whether we could set up our own radio, and he raised his eyebrows, you know how I mean.* Then Ted would trail off, and just when I was ready to torture, beg, or pay him into telling me what our dad had said, he would unwrap his secret knowledge and share it with me like a midnight feast. *He's weakening,* Ted might say. *It's just a matter of time until he says yes.*

"You said you want to know what you're doing here. In this year, in my room." Dylan has a similar air of superior knowledge.

"Well, logic tells us that if you're a ghost, then you're obviously dead. Sorry and all that, Casey."

"Don't apologize," I say. "You didn't kill me."

He grins. "I've got the perfect alibi. You died before I was born."

Something we have in common: silent laughter.

I sober up first. "But exactly how did I die?"

I wish I hadn't asked that question.

There is a creak and then a roar, so loud that it rips me apart. Lightning flashes down through the roof, and a hurricane descends. Dylan exists for an instant, and then he's gone — I'm gone — the real world is gone.

The hurricane spins the pieces of me in black terror just long enough for me to wonder whether I might have died going over Niagara Falls in a barrel, and then I'm dumped, not back into Dylan's room, but somewhere I have been before, and where I least want to be.

Give me the hurricane, leave me in pieces, but not here.

There is no sky here, but the light nearly blinds me. It's white as flamed magnesium. There's a chill in the centre of my being that means fear. What's more, I'm solid, with arms and legs and a body, like when I was alive.

And I'm visible. No, not visible. *Exposed.*

Like a mouse before a hawk under moonlight.

And in front of me? Here it is. The door.

I've been here before. I remember what I'm supposed to do.

I'm supposed to open it. There is no handle on this side. Still, it's up to me to open it.

I watch my hand rise. I have touched this door before. It's cold as stone and thin as a pie pan. It vibrates faintly with the resonance of what waits on the other side. When it starts to

open, a light much more cruel and piercing than this one will slice like a knife through the crack.

I watch my hand move towards the handle. There seems no way to stop the movement. But I've been here before. I've escaped. How?

I touch the handle.

And I remember. Exposed and terrified, I can still be strong.

I know the rule. I can only be forced if I don't refuse. So I shout *no*.

Nothing happens.

I shout it again. The hurricane returns, rips me apart, and throws the pieces into a river of shadow.

Chapter 3

Light filtered in from the windows in the patients' rooms. Morning was rising quickly, and with it came the end of Jamie's shift.

Voices called. PA speakers overhead crackled. Trolley wheels squeaked and bumped along the linoleum floor. The hospital corridors filled with staff dressed in pastel polyester uniforms like her own, and the air filled with smells of disinfectant and breakfast.

Jamie

Her hand was writing her name.

Jamie

The handwriting was her own. She threw the pen down on the computer paper and watched it roll to the floor. It clattered to a stop where the floor met the wall.

Her right hand lay atop the stack of paper in front of her. She watched her fingers for any false move, but they lay as still as if they had never written a word that hadn't sprung from her own mind. And maybe it hadn't. Far more likely she'd dreamed the whole thing.

Still, Jamie was not one to fall asleep on the job. She was young, and in good health for a washed-out creature of the night; what was more, she enjoyed and valued her employment. Nowhere would she be better situated to be invisible to the daylight world. She was harming nobody and doing good. And she needed the money, as everybody in the world needed the money. All in all, it never did to doze off on her shift.

But perhaps, this one night, she'd succumbed, fatigued by the death of G Gordon, a man with whom she'd never spoken, but who turned out to be more important to her than she had first understood. It was possible that, this one night, she had nodded off, chin on hand, and dreamed of writing another person's thoughts all night long. Dreamed of a dead person like G Gordon.

Furthermore, there was her own half-forgotten culture's acceptance of paranormal beings. *You were having a nightmare, little girl.* Her mother's words clicked in her dry mouth, while the crowded, creaking ship tossed on the seas outside Saigon, steering for Hong Kong if they were lucky, or points unknown if they were not. *Wake up, before a ghost enters your dreams.*

Imagination, superstition, the dreaming state. Any of these served to explain her aching hand and her fall into forbidden sleep. None satisfied her. She placed both palms on the printouts on the desk in front of her.

The paper stack sat fatly, dot-matrix print menu side up. *Cottage Pudding. Farmhouse Vegetables. Surprise Custard.* All she had to do was turn the stack over and see for herself: the pages would be empty of all writing except her own sleepy scrawl as she fell, shamefully, asleep.

"Hey, Jamie, space cadet of the night-time shift."

Jamie looked up. Zane the day orderly stood before her: the bold, the beautiful, the built. Each time they met at break of day, Zane, without a word of unkindness, made Jamie feel like bread half-baked and unleavened.

Zane said, "Awaken, starlit Jamie, for the shades of night have fallen away, and we of the sunlit peoples salute you."

"I'm awake. I was a little bleary, that's all." Jamie draped her arm over the two-inch stack of pages on the desktop, like a kid covering her math answers.

Zane said, "You don't have to explain, girl. If I had night shift, I'd spend it snoring behind the mops. Do you want me to toss out that stack of menu printouts, before a nurse gets on my case about it?"

"I'll do it on my way out." Jamie picked up the papers, menu side towards Zane.

Zane peered at the pages. "I never thought it would be so hard to say goodbye to *Surprise Custard*." She snatched an orange from a passing trolley and shared the orange segments with members of staff; the orderly charged with the trolley swore at Zane good-naturedly and passed her a banana.

Zane said, "Remember to smile, dear Jamie. You're a walking glamour puss. You're Myrna Loy."

Jamie was a long way from smiling. The longer she held the papers in her arms, the less certain she was that she had merely dreamed the ghost and his roundhand writing.

She turned to leave, but Zane barred her way. "Anything unusual last night? Alarms? Excursions? Awakenings?"

Jamie hesitated. "We lost G Gordon."

"Not G Gordon. Damn. I liked him crazy well."

"He never woke up."

"They rarely do, but I thought if anybody did, G Gordon would. I liked him for his mane of hair and those carven brows. He lived, that one. He loved, I'd bet my pointiest boots. Why did you like him?"

Jamie considered. "He knew things I wish I knew."

"Small words, big thought." Zane took off an imaginary hat and pressed it to her bosom. "Farewell, G Gordon. Angels sing thee cool jazz to thy rest."

A passing orderly whistled, and Zane whistled back.

"See, Jamie? G Gordon would be the first to say that life goes on. And on that note, now I've caught you, I've got a little matchmaking up my sleeve."

"Please don't trouble." Jamie took a step away.

Zane followed. "I'm relentless with it, so abandon all thought of escape. Get ready for romance, because I have discovered a small office full of terrifying substances in glass tubes, and inside that office, a bookish young urologist who is single."

"Then what if you date him, Zane?"

"I would indeed if I were not gay. Come and meet him. You never know — your nightwing heart might never ache again."

Jamie smiled. "I won't dare ask for so much."

"Ask for more. Step up and get you a life."

Jamie shook her head. She respected urology as a field of study, but romance was impossible. Hers hadn't been much of a marriage, and she might by now be a widow, but the last thing she wanted was to get involved with anybody. For their safety, and for hers.

She peeked at the stack of papers, and saw the word *I* written roundly on the top page. Never in her life had she written so big and oval an *I*. She held the papers tighter against her chest.

"Night-night," Zane joked, as she did every morning. She tossed the banana peel over the heads of several members of staff, a perfect shot into a rolling bin.

Jamie half-hid the stack of paper under her arm, carried it to her locker, and slipped it into her big straw handbag. She shouldered her bag and walked towards the exit. On impulse, she ducked through the emergency waiting room and popped three coins into the coffee machine.

In case of shock, administer hot sweet liquids. She selected *white with sugar.* Coffee in hand, she hurried out through the automatic front doors and stood swaying at the top of the steps to emergency. Coffee splashed on her scrubs and canvas shoes, and she sipped at the cup to bring down the surface level. The five steps down to the path appeared high and warped, as if they'd been drawn with no ruler and a weak perspective. She took her noodle legs down the accessible ramp instead.

To her left, the city's high-rise sprawl, which included her own apartment building; to her right, a small park. The wooded space was lightly used in early spring because trees overhung the concrete benches, most of them dripping from an overnight rain shower. She took the lone dry concrete bench out in the open and set her bag on the seat beside her. The thick corner of the menu printouts stuck out of the top of her bag. She pulled out the stack and turned it over.

What she hoped to find: a few words of her own writing, a bit different from her usual hand because of drowsiness, trailing off as she fell fast asleep at the nurse's desk.

What she found: page after page of large round writing not her own.

She flipped to the middle, and to the end. The pages were filled with a story she hadn't written. She shoved the papers back inside her bag and shifted uncomfortably on the bench. What if she kept the bag shut and got rid of it without further investigation? She took stock of the other contents of her handbag. She could live without the hairbrush and extra socks she kept in it. Here for her convenience stood a trash bin, not twenty feet away, but she hesitated to toss the handbag out. She had an unwelcome feeling that she oughtn't dump it, because of concern for public safety, as if it contained radioactive material or a snake.

"It's only writing," she told her coffee cup.

The morning air was cold and wet, and smelled of ferns and conifers. The concrete spread cold across her shoulders and under her rear. She drank another swig of warm, sweet coffee and held the paper cup against her cheek. She wished for somebody with whom to discuss the night's events. Maria? Zane? But she feared to destroy these pleasant, evolving connections with a bomb of loony ghost talk.

When she was very young, before she and her mother had forsaken Vietnam for a chancy boat on the unforgiving ocean, Jamie's mother would listen to her troubles. She had been trained in Paris as an engineer and would draw flow charts to help Jamie understand her options. *Either this or not, daughter. See what comes of each.* And then she would go out into the rice fields and keep her child safe and fed for one more day.

Either this or not.

Either she had fallen asleep, or she had not.

If she had nodded off, then it was a professional error on her part, and she must not let it happen again. Coffee was the obvious solution, and so long as the drinks machine near her locker was in order, she was set. *Either coffee will work, or it won't.* If coffee let her down, she'd try those caffeine pills again, the ones that made her heart race and her spirit quiver like a Chihuahua.

But, if she had not fallen asleep, and she didn't remember writing page after page in the dark hours of night, then who had written them? Might somebody have come upon her asleep at the desk, taken up pen and paper, filled all these pages, and replaced them before she woke?

She managed to envision a person writing the pages. She pictured it, like a scene in a movie, wherein a shadowy figure crept up on a sleeping orderly to write a story. But what she couldn't imagine was anyone's motivation for doing so.

Further, when she closed her eyes and attempted to believe such a set-up without understanding how it might be, she could not. Raised by an engineer, pushed to reason, she knew better than to disregard a cognitive process. *Better to leave a question unanswered than to cheat one's own mind.*

Might she not continue on with her life without reaching any understanding of what had happened to her? She wouldn't lie, at least not to herself, and say it never happened. All she could do was make a decision never to tell anybody about …

She glanced sideways at the papers in her handbag.

… this.

Jamie gave herself a shake and stood up. She crumpled the empty coffee cup and dropped it into the trash can. With careful movements, she reached through the gap at the top of her straw bag and took hold of the sheaf of paper between finger and thumb, ready to throw it into the trash after the cup if necessary.

No ghost hand reached up to grab her by the wrist. It was over. But it didn't feel over.

She walked briskly towards home. The exercise would help to clear her mind for the day's sleep after the night's alarms. When she woke, she would read the pages she carried in her bag. After which she was free to destroy them.

One good thing about a life without friends or even bookish urologists calling her up and getting to know her, was that she could be cowardly without disappointing people who might otherwise think well of her. The corollary was that she could be brave without endangering anybody. This wasn't the first time she'd made this silent, secret observation.

However, this was certainly the first time that she made it and wondered, despite her love of reason, whether somebody even more invisible than she might be listening.

Casey's story took no more than an hour to read, but the pages jammed with his large writing gave Jamie plenty to think about over the course of her next shift on the wards. To be certain of staying awake through the night, she drank twice as much coffee as usual.

Maria triumphed again at cribbage. "You're not all here, Jamie. I was going to suggest a penny a point, but it would be playing crib against a fish in a barrel."

Jamie apologized. "I'll drink even more coffee, and you can skin me for every penny I have."

"Ha. Your hands are shaking. Lay off the coffee."

"We'll see. Tell me this: did I yawn during our game?"

Maria shook her head. "Play again?"

"I'll come back later if I can. Meantime, you might want to please your doctors by getting some sleep."

"An unlikely scenario."

"Have you always had trouble sleeping?"

"Ha. No."

"Is it the noises that keep you awake?"

"If only."

"What, then?"

Maria shuffled her cards. "I'm pretty sure I know what my tests will reveal."

"Look at you, with your excellent colour. Nobody looks as healthy as you do. Certainly not me."

"No wonder you're an orderly. You'd make a terrible doctor. *You look fantastic. Put away that stool sample and go home.*"

"Maybe the doctors will say just that."

"Then I'll pack up my cards and go home."

"That would make me happy."

"Thanks so much." Maria rolled her eyes. "Would you like to know what would please me?"

"Tell me."

"I'd jump for joy to see you leave your shadow realm here in the hospital night shift and get out into the world. Travel, fall in love. Make some big mistakes."

"Sounds terrifying."

"*She joked.*"

"A little bit terrifying. Anyway, I'm perfectly capable of making mistakes working the night shift."

"Ha. You're young and lovely. In the name of middle age,

don't waste your daylight hours. Leave the night to insomniacs and the sleeping people. Leave night-time to the ghosts."

Silence hung between them for a moment. The pages of Casey's night-time writing Jamie had read the day before returned to her in a wash of darkness and dread. She wanted to explain to Maria that being a ghost and being young were not mutually exclusive.

A buzzer broke the silence. Both women looked towards the nurses' station, which stood empty. Somebody needed Jamie.

Maria shuffled her cards. "Go and do your thing. Leave me to mine. It's a little-known fact that if a patient wins three games of solitaire in a row, all her tests will come back negative."

Jamie did her thing. She gave ice chips to the thirsty patient who had buzzed, visited the coma patients, mopped, and dusted. When she discovered Maria asleep at last, she tidied her cards away into her bedside stand.

Zane appeared with the morning sunlight and handed Jamie an apple. Stuck to it was a sticky note with a phone number, or rather an extension number. Jamie guessed it would connect her with the urology department.

"Zane, you're the best, but it's not the right time in my life for phoning up men. I'll eat the apple, though."

"Life? You're aware of its existence, then?" Zane inclined her head. "Maybe stop at a supermarket on the way home. You need to get you some of that."

"I'll put it on my shopping list. See you Monday."

"Girl, do something to spoil yourself this weekend. You look what my grandmother called *peaked*."

"I'll see what I can find."

Jamie was halfway to her locker when Zane called out to her. "Hey, Jamie, I just remembered: if you step up, you'll get yourself a life."

Jamie took her coat and bag out of her locker. *Tell that to Casey. I don't think stepping up to anything would get a life for a dead man.*

She paused with her coat half on and her straw handbag on the floor between her feet. It still contained the stack of pages covered with ghost writing.

Either this or not, daughter. Jamie desired above all things to show the pages to her mother and hear how she might explain their seemingly inexplicable provenance. But her mother had long ago left her, faded out of life after a pirate attack on that noisy, tossing ship out of Saigon twelve years before.

The engineer's daughter would have to decide on her own what to believe.

Or, with apologies to her mother—who, even in their time of slavery in the rice fields, had always been certain of her choices and acted on them—Jamie must decide whether she was actually capable of deciding on a number of questions.

Do I believe in ghosts?

If I do believe, was Casey one?

As if she'd opened a box upside down, more questions tumbled out.

Should I pack my bags now and leave behind my job, my apartment, and the scene of the impossible visitation?

Should I stay, though, because orderlies are thin on the ground, and orderlies who choose night shift are rare indeed?

Then,

Is it too soon to run from my in-laws?

Is it even possible to run away from hell too soon?

Her mother had taught her to act. The criminal family who had adopted Jamie upon her arrival in this country had taught her to think before she acted. But what both had taught her best was to escape.

To disappear. Like a ghost. Like Casey.

She must put on her coat, walk outside, and think. Before she left her locker, she took her few personal belongings — a bag of throat lozenges, a scarf left over from wintertime, a bottle of prescription cough syrup — in case she never returned. She didn't need them now that it was springtime, but she was determined that nobody else would clean up after her.

Also, she was painstaking about not leaving behind clues.

§

In our next issue of Pulp Literature, *Jamie struggles to stay out of sight in the living world, while ghostly visitations push her further out of hiding, into danger of discovery and recapture.*

OCTAVIER

Nat Kishchuk

Nat Kishchuk began creative writing in 2019, after too many years of writing something completely different. Her fiction and creative non-fiction have appeared in carte blanche, The Rumen, Crow and Cross Keys, Yolk Literary Journal, and Andromeda Spaceways. Nat's secret ambition is to write speculative fiction that advances social justice by shifting perceptions of unacceptable realities. 'Octavier' is about the migrant crisis, in homage to Mohsin Hamid's magic doors in Exit West. For the musical inspirations, Nat is indebted to Joon Oh Kim, the most versatile of accompanists; and Jeffrey Stonehouse and Eli Saab, flautists extraordinaire.

OCTAVIER

Front lights. Followspot on one tall microphone. Steinway. No chairs but my bench. Felty murmurings of a winter-dressed audience, a full house, deep. I've learned to read the room before I even try to surmise what I'm wearing, usually some clueless black.

OK, then, this time I will be accompanying a soloist in a professional performance. Already a lot of information, ruling out several hundred thousand possibilities. What instrument? Voice or something played standing: many other possibilities eliminated. What repertoire? I step onstage, take my seat, and place my feet.

The octaves always spit me right to the moment I must enter the stage — of course, because it's always exactly on the hour. I can't look behind me to see who I will be playing for. I've missed any program presentation and have only these few moments to figure out what my fingers and feet need to do. This is the hardest part, though. Once I get started, the rest of it is quite predictable. Hands on lap, multiplicities X potentialities.

Applause now. The soloist is entering. It's not a huge burst of pent-up adoration, so not a top-three star, but greeted warmly — perhaps their home town. Throat clearing: a teeny tell. It's a vocalist, contralto, therefore most likely pre-twenty-first classical. The hundred or so prospects array in my mind, and I flex my fingers. A long blue dress walks past, takes centre stage. She turns to nod at me. It's Forrester. Ergo, we're probably still in Montréal, it's probably back in 1982, and I'm for sure channelling Newmark. I straighten up and position myself for the opening bars of Haydn's *Arianna a Naxos*.

At first, it was scary-strange, then just pesky.

Then it ruined my life.

It started early in my second semester at the Conservatoire. After a few crazy trips, I got what was going on and realized it probably wasn't other people's normal: just another way I'm special. Even though it kept happening, after the performance I'd always get shunted directly back to whatever it was I had been doing, like jamming with the Roxhams or playing Minecraft or doodling in some dumb chromaticism class.

Forrester finishes the encore then gestures to me. I make my bow, dreading the dump back. Oddly, the entrances are never physically hard, but the departures are disorienting: my brain, in thrall to the reverberating last notes, is never ready to leave.

And here I am, back in the ballet studio, accompanying the Junior Fours. I can tell this is my 2024 reality — in fact, one of my part-time paying gigs, because, first of all, it's the middle of the hour, and, second, the teacher is scowling at me. "Tempo!" she hisses. The bullies in the group try to model her glare. The anxious ones try to displace even fewer molecules, their gaunt features pinchy.

By the end of the semester, I had figured out that the trigger was a combination of seeing the time display an exact hour and hearing a precisely tuned octave. I'd played around with it a little, testing the parameters. Fifty-nine seconds after the hour took me away, but sixty-one did not. One octave only, played within those sixty seconds on any one or more instruments but mine. The notes have to be in tune within plus or minus eleven cents, but more off-key than that, no go.

When I was a bit fed up or had been composing too hard to enjoy the challenge, I only took jobs accompanying solo voices or winds, and tried to stay away from those ultra-contemporaries and their multiphonics. It still happened occasionally; as a child I'd been obsessive about knowing the exact hour all the time, waking up in the night to check it. When anxious — *id est*, always — I couldn't fully repress the reflex. Plus, hanging at the Conservatoire meant that inevitable octaves would crash out of the practice rooms along the yellow-puke corridors, whether they were the right notes or not.

In short, I'd sort of gotten used to it and could kind of control it. I believe this helped me cope after my devastating loss: I could mostly scrape the longing, that dark sweet caramel oozing toward my heart, back to the edges of my consciousness.

So now I'm on one of those tiresome stages where my job is to play the set piece exactly the same way over and over again. This time flute, the Chaminade of-fucking-course *Concertino*. There are so many recordings of auditions like this that I almost don't bother searching my memory for this exact one. Nose-peery jury at their table in the pit, faces aghast by default. I give each quivery flautist a little smile and lean in. If nothing else, these out-of-time experiences give me an extra chance to practise my so-called social skills.

At the start of the third kid's *più animato e agitato* section, recollection arcs from fingers to ears to brain: I've accompanied this musician before. I start to pay attention, but it's not true of any of what seems like several hundred others.

Pitched back to my present body, I'm still in room 2405, waiting for Cesaria and KC, our leader. Bohdan, the newest member of the Roxham Roadies Quartet, is already practising the Messiaen, which is what we are supposed to be working on that day. While warming up on frantic contrary arpeggios, I try to remember where I had played for that flautist before. As though it could be a clue. Because if I can be in the same space with one random musician more than once, maybe it could happen with Dominik, too. My longing suddenly fixes, caramel crystallized into craving. The practice goes badly.

Later that night, alone in my room, I can't help but strop my ardour by revisiting that traverse. I was already a little in love with his music after listening to the Berliner's *New World,* to the point that I considered wasting some time to look him up. To be prepared for anything, I need to listen to everything I possibly can, but just once; my memory is so far infallible, and anything more is extraneous. But I fall in love with lots of music, and just put him on the mythical when-I-have-time list. Onstage, when I realized it was Dominik Wollenweber, principal English horn of the Berlin Philharmonic, in recital, I was merely pleased. Whoever I had showed up as was familiar to him — so surely Kirichenko, and surely we were in Leipzig. I expected to enjoy myself.

Then, just the one nod, and I was draining into those eyes, that grey-green candour. I tried to focus while liquefying.

It was his hands that aroused me most. A once-pianist's fingers, I'm sure, there's an action to the metacarpophalangeal that's characteristic, IMHO. Caressing the length of his English horn, a Lorée to be precise. During the Sibelius *Swan* with the totally forgettable cellist, my lighting was off and I could half-turn to watch. My guts were churning, my thighs were shaking, my lips itched.

I was flung away upon the opening notes of the unaccompanied encore—the *Shepherd's Song* from Tristan, a lament I wouldn't have survived. I knew I would never be the same. No one had ever felt a love like this before. I was ruined.

The only way I could live with the longing was to convince myself I would never see Dominik again, that each time-trip was unique. This I had mostly managed. When it was unbearable, his YouTube recordings were my blow. I had accepted this as the tragedy of my life.

But now, this premise is broken. How can I get to be in the same space with him again? Then how can I stay there? And get those hands on me? Dominik-nik-nik. It all seems so unsurmountable. I cry myself to sleep.

The next day brings resolve. Until I can figure out a strategy, I'll get more exposure; maybe some pattern will emerge that I haven't yet spotted. I sign up for a jillion accompaniment jobs, master classes, pickup ensembles, auditions. No composer alive after 1850, all conventional octave-full classics. I basically live in the Conservatoire with my eyes riveted to the placid moonface clocks. As I expect, I'm thrown into theatres and studios and auditoriums and church halls and opera houses. I play for bassoonists and baritones, harpists, clarinettists and violists and, under a millstone of misery, another English hornist. Once, incredibly, I'm the *pianiste-répétiteur* at a music camp I attended as a kid. I wonder if *OCTAVIER 2009* is still ballpointed on the plywood of my practice cubby.

It never happens again that I'm playing with someone for a second time.

I've just been popped back into the ballet studio, Junior Five this time, when I notice something is hanging on to my left ankle. This was the fifth extra-temporal excursion today, discombobulation exponentiated by disappointment, so I'm not sure it's really there. Fortunately, the Heintzman upright is angled so that no one else can see it. I check the mirror wall while continuing to pound out *EK Nachtmusik*. It's a person, small and dark, huddled half-under the piano, head on one arm. I raise my heel. It tightens its grip.

I'm sure I had no such appendages when I got here. I was on the verge of being late, as it was seconds after 4:00 pm and I'd been dawdling past the chamber music studios hoping to be struck by octaves. The only place I've been since entering the ballet room is the E Glenn Giltz Auditorium at SUNY Plattsburgh circa 2017, happy accident of a Wagnerian 'vaft' through the closing door at 4:00:53. This person must have travelled back with me. While Madame is haranguing on crabby hands, I surreptitiously pick up my coat from the chair next to me and drop it over the person. It snuffles, and snuggles closer to my foot.

When the rehearsal ends, I stand by the piano, pretending to read scores on my tablet while the dansters gaggle off, then crouch to get a better look.

It's a child, possibly a girl about nine, although I try to avoid categorical data. She's a soft lump of oversize clothes: bunchy socks stuffed into muddy adult runners, bits of twig and leaf dotting a hooded sweatshirt knotted firmly under her chin. She looks at me, then reaches out her arms.

"Khto tse?" Bohdan asks as I sit the kid down on a creaky black folding chair. She kind of melts into the seat, her hands sliding down my arms. This was the only place I could think of to take her: down the hall and up the two flights of stairs to 2405. Bohdan's question answers one of mine: I'm not the only one who can see her.

"Sister's kid," I mumble.

"Aha. Your neffooo," Bohdan says, proud of his fresh vocabulary.

"Yeah," I say.

"Hello," Bohdan says to the kid, who smiles, impish, and says "Hola! Hola!" Another question answered.

When Cesaria and KC arrive, I borrow all the coats to make a kind of a nest on a carpet in the corner. She sleeps through the whole practice, only peeking watchful eyes over the edge of the coat pile once, when Bohdan pretends to scold the rest of us for playing so well as to eclipse his solo.

After practice, I take her to the bathroom and, after establishing she's hungry through miming—my Spanish is by now almost extinct—down to the main-floor cafeteria to buy her the fattest panini of those left in the case. She eats some, working top down, and stows the rest in pockets. We hang out there, and for some reason I keep talking to her in this low, reassuring voice I didn't know I could do. I point out where the garbages are kept and emptied, the fridges that can be glimpsed through the side door to the kitchen, and then, on a little tour outside, past the door that can get someone in or out of the building after hours if they leave a pebble on the threshold. My intentions are not clear to me. I show her how to get back to 2 4 0 5, which the Roxhams have on semi-permanent reservation, and leave her there while I go trolling for consonance.

I do keep checking in every once in a while all night; she's just sleeping, but once she waggles her hand at me before a cat-like re-burrow.

When I get back in the morning, finally having gone home to doze for a couple of jagged hours, she's gone. I acknowledge I'm feeling something about this. I launch into today's schedule: recital season is coming up, and I've several accompaniment practices, ballet sessions for Junior Four and Senior Two, plus a new big band, the Darién Gaps, that KC has convinced me to try out for. Plenty of opportunity to get slung through time and space.

She's gone, but a new one comes, this time tagging along as I depart the Sillery Singers' 2 0 2 2 Christmas concert—what the fuck is figgy pudding anyway?—and then, on each trip, there's another. The quartet starts contributing food and old clothes and blankets and don't ask questions. Honour among musicians, I guess. The children keep joining then leaving me, a steady stream through my times and spaces.

Once, on a rainy evening, I re-glimpse the first girl, shepherding an even smaller person out that back door. A shadow of three adults is waiting behind a tree on the other side of Hotel-de-Ville. One lunges across to pick up the littler one, hugs him wholly and kisses him all over. I'm surprised to feel my eyes stinging. They all look at me and make the slightest nod. I recognize it: musician code for 'we are here now and we are ready.'

I pursue my search for Dominik, but I'm starting to feel hopeless. I blame myself for not having paid more attention to the circumstance of our brief connection, for not having acted instantly. I fantasize that as he reaches the jubilant *fine* of Françaix's *Allegro giocoso,* I launch myself at his left ankle, to stay where I so certainly belong.

One day, I hear him, I'm sure, in the Conservatoire's recital hall. This could be real! This could happen! A guesting gig, an artist in residence, oh, dare I hope, a job audition. But, dumbass, of course not. I'm skulking outside when the pianist and not-Dominik leave, laughing. I acknowledge I'm losing my mind.

Then it stops. First, the *rio* of migrants trickles, then dries up. The last ones were really thin, and a couple were covered in scratches. Then, no more octaving. I get Bohdan to experiment on me, doublestopping the whole violin range, without saying exactly why. Exactly nothing.

I don't miss those trips, really. I acknowledge I will never see Dominik again. That feels like a flume from my heart to oblivion. But now that they're not happening, I wonder why they did. A flake of the universe's disintegration? A test-quest that I may have passed, or failed? Or maybe nothing to do with me?

KC, whose chord progressions sometimes sizzle me, talks me into a jam night that I end up kind of liking, then into a steady gig in their jazz ensemble. I learn, not from KC, that they used to play English horn before the clarinet. The ensemble is called the Dover Straights, and they practise in room 1505. One night after practice, KC and I find ourselves wrapped up in each other in the pile of coats and blankets that has never left 2405. The pile smells like woodsmoke and diesel. KC smells like cardamom. I ask why they played English horn. They say, "C'mon, you know this. Same as a lot of English hornists. I wasn't good enough on oboe to get first chair." I ask why they don't play English horn any more. "Fucking double reeds," they say.

A day not long after that, I'm hanging out, waiting for KC to finish an alt-tonal theory class, watching the hallway clock tick 2:00 pm, when there is a slight space in my head, a syncope rest beat. I almost don't have time to realize that it has always preceded a time shift. I do have time to realize that there was no octave in what I was hearing — it was your basic major seventh, that old jazz staple. And here I go again.

North African fusion. Backup to a bald oudist whom I don't know. It's not the repertoire that unnerves me — I will just have a lot to listen to — it's that I'm not the accompanist, I'm part of the band. Oh so happily, this is a recording session and has come with charts, copyright 1991. I fumble as best I can, stealing clues from the formidable bassist, but get the sense that I'm not on the album credits. When the oudist stalks out, that familiar swoosh and—

I'm back in 1505 with the Dovers. A child is clinging to my ankle. Her size and posture aren't so different from all the previous ones, but I know right away from her colours and clothes that she's from another part of the world, maybe another century. Little nail-moons are scoring my skin. In some left-hand rest bars, I put my hand on her head, hold it there for a moment. She loosens her grasp but still hangs on.

I look up. KC is watching me. They give me that musician nod. We play.

THE NEWTONBROOK NINJA

Preston Lang

Preston Lang is a small, honest writer based in Ontario. His fiction has appeared in Grain, N + 1, Queen's Quarterly, and The Best American Mystery Stories 2019 and 2021.

The Newtonbrook Ninja

Matthew started dating the ninja in January. She called herself Tammy. Cunning and athletic, she always wore black, but so did every other smart young woman on the subways of New York. On their first date, they ate ramen, and he told her about himself: originally from Canada, currently working as an independent IT consultant, afraid of snakes and turtles. She was less forthcoming about her background. Instead she ranked her favourite spices, from green cardamom down to mahlab, and she described a few simple exercises you could do to increase your grip strength. When the cheque came, Matthew accidentally knocked his water glass off the table. Tammy deftly snatched it out of the air and placed it back in front of him without spilling a drop.

"Hey, are you a ninja or something?" he asked with a little laugh. She changed the subject.

Later they kissed in Union Square Park, not far from the statue of Gandhi. He found that she had almost no taste even though she'd just consumed two bowls of hoisin-drenched ramen.

Matthew went back a second time, a third time, kissing her on the neck, the chin, then to the mouth again. She took a step back.

"Actually, I am a ninja," she said. "Are you sure you want to see me again?"

The moment of vulnerability was almost impossibly poignant. He wanted to see her every day for the rest of his life.

She texted him in the morning and said she would be busy for the next three days, but she wanted to get together on Wednesday. Again, she gave him an out: *Or have you changed your mind about me?* There was clearly a warning in the question, but Matthew was completely smitten. Besides, they actually had a lot in common: they were both independent contractors, lovers of noodles and moonlight.

She began to stay over at his place three or four nights a week, though sometimes she'd disappear for days without a word. He tried to have her meet his friends: university buddies and a few of the guys from his volleyball league. Somehow it never happened. There would always be a last-minute cancellation, a venue shut down for fire code violations, a flash flood halting traffic through the tunnels. When asked, Matthew found that he had trouble describing her physical appearance accurately. He assumed she was a young, Japanese American woman, but in February, she took a job that required her to spend two weeks posing as a deli owner, a stout Armenian man in his fifties. At night, she'd stay in disguise, hold him tight, and demand that he call her Tigran. It was exciting and mind-expanding, but he was glad to have her back as *Tammy* by March.

For most of the winter, he'd been trying to collect from a client who owed him two thousand dollars for a job in December.

"You know how it is," he said to Tammy.

"How what is?"

"Freelancing. They don't pay, so you have to keep sending really cordial emails: *Hey, just checking up again on the status of my invoice. Hope you're having a great day.*"

"No, I've never had to do that."

"Really?"

"Not once."

"Well, it's a headache for a lot of us."

She gave an almost imperceptible nod as if they'd just reached a tacit understanding.

The next morning, he replayed the conversation in his head. When he'd told the story, he'd mentioned the client by name twice: Jack Rosner. Tammy's nod had meant—what? That she understood he'd asked her for help?

He called the client—straight to voicemail. He looked up the address of the company, but it was just a PO box. Finally he was able to find Jack Rosner's home address in Astoria. Matthew took the subway out there then climbed to the top floor of a six-storey walkup.

Jack was at home in sweats and flip-flops, blasting Drake from expensive speakers. Matthew introduced himself as the man who'd saved his website. Then he asked for what he was owed.

"You came to my home?"

"You really need to pay this. If you don't pay—it's going to be really bad for you."

Jack tried to stare him down for a moment.

"I got a little behind on paperwork. I'll write you a cheque. Jesus."

Matthew took the cheque right to the bank and texted Tammy: *Whaddaya know? Client paid in full. Maybe not such a bad guy after all.*

That night, they went ice skating in Prospect Park. Matthew was an unspectacular skater, but most New Yorkers were impressed by how well he moved on the ice. Tammy had never skated before, and he wondered if this was the sort of skill a ninja would quickly master. The rentals were blue and red. He could tell she didn't like that they weren't black, didn't like that she had no choice in the matter.

"You went to his place," she said.

"Whose place?"

"You really thought I'd kill him? Just because he didn't pay you?"

It was senseless to try to pretend with her; she had ways of knowing things.

"I wasn't sure," he said. "I didn't want anything to happen to him."

"You didn't want blood on your *own* hands?"

"That's not it."

She pulled the laces tight, a perfect bow on top.

"You can't judge me," she said.

"I don't judge you."

"And you can't ever ask who my targets are."

"Do you always have a … *target?*"

"What do you mean?"

"Do you ever just, I don't know, gather information?"

"This — what you just said now — this feels like a judgement."

She stood up and teetered slightly.

"I don't want to skate."

She sat down and began to undo the laces.

"But we already paid for the —"

"Let's see a film."

Tammy liked movies. She seemed at ease in the darkness of a theatre, and she wasn't picky. Romcoms, teen horror, it was all fine with her. She relaxed inside a story. He'd hold the popcorn and reach for her hand during romantic moments.

For her birthday, he took her to see *The Black Mask*, a highly regarded indie picture directed by Katie Sato, a twenty-something auteur from British Columbia.

"In this film, we finally move past cliché and fantasy and take an honest look at the themes and issues relevant to the contemporary ninja," wrote the critic for the *New York Times*.

Matthew enjoyed the first half hour. To him, it was very real and very human. The conversations between the ninja and her half-sister felt raw and honest. But when he looked over at Tammy, she was seething. Finally, when the on-screen ninja laid out her credo, Tammy stood and left the theatre. Matthew followed out through the lobby and onto the street.

"Why did you think I'd like that?" she asked.

All he could do was weakly parrot the *Times*. "I thought it was a very sensitive depiction of the issues and concerns of a contemporary ninja."

"How would you know the issues and concerns of a contemporary ninja?"

He felt a wave of shame. He hadn't even considered that she might not like the movie, let alone find it offensive. And while he had more insight into the mind of a ninja than almost any other man in New York, the gulf between what he thought he knew and reality was enormous.

"It was disgusting," she said. "We don't talk that way. We don't act that way."

He nodded, almost tried to take her hand, then decided against it.

"Can I ask what *are* the issues that are most important to you, as a ninja?" he said.

She pointed at the poster in the window — a ninja looking mournfully at her reflection in the ocean.

"Anything but this."

"Sometimes . . . sometimes I don't know what's important to you. I don't know because you don't tell me. You don't tell me what your problems are."

He didn't need every detail, but he wanted to know her anxieties, her dreams. He longed to hear how she felt about all the stealth and all the complexities of her moral code.

"You want to know my problems?" she asked.

"Yes. Give me anything."

She shrugged, struggling for something to tell him.

"As a ninja, do you have any idea how high my insurance premiums are?" she asked.

"No. Tell me."

"It's inhuman, how we're treated." She now had an edge of real indignation in her voice. "If I'm injured by gunshot, that's covered by my insurance. But if I'm injured leaping out of the way of a bullet, that is *not* covered. I'm better off letting the bullet hit me."

"Yeah, a lot of these policies don't make much sense. I'm a freelancer too, so I understand — "

"No, you don't. You don't understand. You can't understand."

She didn't stay the night; she didn't even kiss him when they came to her subway station. He couldn't sleep; he was sick with regret and self-blame. But she'd also tripped a wire in his brain and reminded him that he had a superpower of his own.

First he researched just how high her premiums could be. On a Reddit thread, someone called Shuriken420 claimed to be paying 3,6 o o dollars a month. *With an eight grand deductible. Ughhhh.* Most commenters decried this as a lie and questioned whether Shuriken4 2 o was really a ninja in the first place, but Matthew found the account compelling. He would do whatever it took to keep Tammy. Would a chef not cook to keep his love? Would a singer not croon to revive fading affections?

Matthew possessed the ability to transform any American into a permanent resident of Canada. He could endow them with quality health insurance through a simple ritual — the sacrament of marriage.

For the next three weeks he didn't see Tammy. She sent him one terse text: *on a job.* It was agony. He constantly checked his phone and scoured the news for creative murders of high-value targets. Then finally, one Tuesday, she fell in step with him just as he came out of the Christopher Street subway station.

"We have to talk," she said.

"Absolutely, yes."

But he feared her tone. They found an outdoor café and drank tea. There was something ritualistic about the way she cooled the beverage — this was an ending.

"We're very different people," she said. "When we met, I thought we could figure out a way to make this work."

No, he had to stop this.

"Can I just say one thing, make one suggestion?" he asked.

"What?"

"Marry me."

"Marry you?"

"I love you, and I want to be with you. We'll move to Toronto."

He described how all her insurance problems would be solved. He made it sound simple and golden. Of course, he knew it could take a year for her to get OHIP, and he didn't mention that dental wasn't covered. She'd have to adjust to a new city, a different transit system, possibly even a tighter market for silent assassins. He was a little less than honest, but this was the only arrow in his quiver.

"I promise you: it can work. We can work."

He saw the subtle tilt in her eyebrows. He'd surprised her with both passion and logic.

"You could leave New York?" she asked.

"Yes, I could."

In fact, he'd started to feel homesick recently. He would happily leave New York behind for Toronto and Tammy. As a freelancer, it would be simple for him. Neither of them said anything for nearly a minute. Finally Tammy spoke.

"I could kill both your parents, drain them of blood, then pose them in deck chairs on their front lawn."

"Why would you do that?"

"I'm saying I could. Do you understand me?"

"No."

"Remember in that ... *movie* you took me to? The way they described a ninja code, things we couldn't do?"

"Yes."

"What I need you to understand is that there's nothing I couldn't do if I had to."

"I understand that."

He wasn't sure that he did, but he said it with conviction.

"We'll go to Toronto for two weeks," she said. "I need to see if I like it."

"Of course. Absolutely."

"If I don't like it, I'm not staying."

"There are other cities in Canada."

"Not in my industry, no."

Was this true? It seemed like Montréal would've had enough work for one more competent blade. And while the idea of a Calgary ninja or a Winnipeg ninja was patently ridiculous, there were certainly people who needed to be killed in Vancouver. But this was the wrong way of looking at it. This again was Matthew thinking he understood more about Tammy's life than she did. He had no choice but to rely on the power and charm of the 416.

September is Toronto's best month. The city is mild and green, but it buzzes with the possibilities of a new season. Matthew showed Tammy all the secrets of the TTC — *see how clean our subways are.* He took her to a little hole in the wall where the most amazing samosas were ten dollars a dozen. They looked through the schedule of the international film festival and found intriguing new movies from Belgium and Taiwan.

On the evening of their thirteenth day in town, they ate takeout jerked chicken on a bench by the lake.

"I can live here," she said.

"Will you marry me?"

He'd bought a ring the night they left New York. Nothing flashy or expensive, no stone, just a silver band.

"Yes, I will marry you." She smiled shyly as he slipped the ring on her finger. "But I can't wear jewellery."

"Just wear it for tonight. Please."

He began to search real-estate listings before she'd finished eating. He wanted a little outdoor space, and he knew she needed a basement with enough room to swing around a katana. If they were going to buy, they might even have to think about extra space, light and airy, that could grow from nursery to bedroom.

When Matthew woke up the next morning, he noticed that Tammy was still wearing his ring. She did a series of complicated stretching exercises then went out on a bikeshare to explore. He read the morning news. Katie Sato, director of *The Black Mask*, had won the critics' choice award for her new film, *Code*, a story of love and betrayal among young tech workers. But very early that morning, her body was found, lifeless, drained of blood, leaning against the brick edifice of the Canadian Tire on Dufferin Street.

MASQUERADE

Wiley Wei-Chiun Ho

Wiley Wei-Chiun Ho *writes short stories, personal essays, and memoir. Her work has appeared in various magazines, journals, and anthologies. 'Masquerade' offers a peek beneath the guises we inhabit, visible and otherwise. It won the 2020 Federation of BC Writers BC-Yukon Short Story Contest. When dodging her desk, Wiley can be found growing Asian vegetables in her front yard or hugging trees in her backyard.*

Masquerade

We see each other infrequently now, usually at your parties.
Or whenever you need a good cry on my shoulder.

You adore fancy parties, cooking for everyone, being mistaken for a woman of leisure with all the time in the world to make dinner for twelve or more. I know better than anyone you're not a trophy wife, despite your pearl-lacquered nails and perfectly toned body, which you've wrapped tonight in a champagne-coloured gown, the plunging neckline outlined in angora.

I see you've invited new friends this evening, and their plus-ones. As you gradually bring out — like fresh canapés — little details about yourself throughout the evening, these acquaintances will be genuinely surprised to learn that you're a single mom. How, besides a busy career, you make time for bake sales, sports games, the arts, and — of course — friendship. At this, you catch my eye even though I'm standing apart from the others, raise your glass of sparkling water, and send me a wink. You introduce me as your oldest friend, leaving 'oldest' to interpretation. You don't mention how far back we go. Or the rehab.

Your expensively dressed guests turn to take stock of me. Loose grey hair, faded sweater, saggy pants. I can tell, from their slightly bemused looks, that they are surprised we are friends.

I tolerate the smirks because I have dressed for myself, despite your warning it would be a dressy affair. It's my protest costume, a subtle middle finger at the one-percenters masquerading as the middle class, the put-together pretending to be all together. I know that you — the flying phoenix tonight in your resplendent dress — grudgingly admire this about me. We know each other, after all.

I am so proud of how far you've come, how high you've clambered from those bottomless nights gripping the toilet, retching and shivering uncontrollably, bawling you would never do it again. Those pre-dawn phone calls when you bled out your anaemic heart, your voice a cracked whisper in my ear, trying not to wake your sleeping daughter dropped off for the weekend by your ex. I yelled at you then. I implored you to keep your seams together so you wouldn't lose your daughter. *Trust me. If you lose your child, you will never forgive yourself.* I have watched you transform, bit by bit, marshalling the madness in a new direction, into a different addiction. You went from getting high to getting promotions, from a rented basement to a penthouse suite. I know that I have become the single incongruity in your life. Yet you hold on to me like cool porcelain. A touchstone.

Tonight, your place feels like a gala reception. The living room is an eruption of fresh flowers, hothouse beauties in reds and purples to resuscitate the hibernating pulse of winter. A jazz trio massages the air from a corner. Tables are laden with finger food: baby quiches dusted with paprika, rosettes of prosciutto, spears of grilled asparagus, cheeses hard and soft flown directly from Europe. A forest of green wine bottles inhabits the granite island, their grown-up labels facing the world. No inferior grape here.

The doorbell chimes again, and you pull me with you towards the door. More guests arriving. Blinding smiles, half-kisses, introductions. "Welcome, please make yourselves at home. Allow me to introduce you to my oldest friend." This is my cue. Curving my lips into a smile, I extend a damp palm. Over and over again.

Pulling me aside, you ask what I think so far. I gush that the place looks gorgeous, that you look lovely. I know how much work you've put in. *No, no,* you laugh, tilting your head towards your new man, who is leaning against the fireplace, chatting with a group of his tribesmen all in the uniform of the sports jacket.

I do not say that he looks like X or that he sounds like Y. Or am I confusing him with Z? It's not only their names I'm forgetting but also their faces. The preternaturally well-preserved faces of the distinguished gents I've met across your threshold are blending together. Tanned visages creased by midday golf and convertible coupes. Clean-shaven and cologned, their gazes are accustomed to holding prolonged eye contact. Their bodies attend the gym, but their generous torsos betray a weakness for late-night scotch. They have hobbies from lifestyle magazines at the doctor's office, pursuits involving powerful engines or large sails. They seem pretentious, the lot of them, unexamined and dull, ideologies that end with tax receipts. But I don't wish to cause a scene tonight. The last time I came clean, you snapped and said what did I know about success or love? I haven't forgotten.

You are looking expectantly at me now. I know what you want from me, even though it is not what you need.

"He seems like a great guy," I say, popping a tiny quiche into my mouth. "Handsome." I sputter flakes.

You smile gratefully, squeeze my arm, and glide back to your guests.

The room drones with elegant chatter. There is a great deal of talk about travel to exotic locales off the beaten path — if only slightly. Your new beau is saying, "Can't be too far from a decent winery, though, can you?"

Keeping my eye-roll in check, I edge towards the stand of expensive bottles, find the cranberry juice you've tucked behind for me, and pour a large goblet. Your new man appears alongside, looking for a Barolo.

"How are you enjoying the party?" he asks, like he owns the place. Without waiting for a response, he says, "You know, you're lucky to have a friend like her."

I know the subtext of his words because I am clearly a charity case. Drawing a full breath, I turn to give him my best smile, showcase my fake front teeth. "Yes, you too."

I sip my juice and wait for him to talk about himself, which he does. I have to bite my tongue to resist inquiring after his sick Afghan hound or his rare knife collection or whether his son has graduated from Princeton, because really, he could be X, Y, or Z. Figuring I should say something, I ask about his business.

He snorts and says didn't he just finish explaining he sold his company? Then he lets out a hearty guffaw that suggests he is willing to be magnanimous because I am his lover's friend.

"Looks like someone's had a bit to drink," he offers but cannot keep his eyes from skimming over my shapeless clothes like I'm the balance sheet of a bankrupt company. He donates a smile and saunters back to the glitterati.

From across the room, you catch my eye. It has not escaped your notice that your new man and I have just had an exchange. You look so hopeful, like a starlet waiting to be called onstage for her award, so I raise my glass in a salute to your obvious success.

I know, in a few weeks, you will be weeping on my shoulder again. And I will rub your back, make soothing sounds. I will try telling you the truth again. That this one will not last, just like the previous clones. That men who care about power and glamour don't care for vulnerability. After the initial weeks of romance and hedonistic sex, after you finally remove the flawless layers, what remains will curdle the man's interest. Your raw need will send him stumbling out of your bedroom with vague promises to call later. But, like the others, he won't, because you will have revealed too much. Despite appearances, you and I are alike. Ashes don't transform into birds. And, you're wrong, I do know something about love. Isn't that why I'm your oldest friend?

For now, though, it's time for me to leave. I have had my fill of bedazzlement and fool's gold. As I pull on my coat, you walk over to say goodnight. There is a tightness about your face.

"I hope the evening hasn't been too tedious?" You say this rhetorically, which makes me smile. A glimmer of you has appeared, and I wrap my arms around this old ally, but I can smell the new man on your skin.

You open the door for me and ask again. "What do you really think of him?"

Looking into your apprehensive eyes, I catch myself reflected there. Have I been too protective—watching and listening but not understanding? When did I forget that recovery is a long and unsparing process? Somewhere a bird flutters among the ashes. It occurs to me that hope is yet another addiction.

When I answer, there is conviction in my voice. "I think he's perfect."

THE JACK WHYTE STORYTELLER'S AWARD

Trish Gauntlett

Trish lives in North Vancouver and works as a writer and editor. She's written two novels, The Gods of Thought and Memory and The Scales of Anubis, *as well as poetry and short fiction.* 'The Ice Road' *was chosen by judge Diana Gabaldon as a runner-up in the 2023 Jack Whyte Storyteller Award. It evokes a place close to Trish's heart — Canada's north.*

The Ice Road

Two weeks out, I dream we are driving across the ice bridge, dream it cracks and roars, dream we race the widening gap to the other side of the Mackenzie River.

It's winter, it's my seventieth birthday, and my husband and I are going to drive the legendary Dempster Highway, 737 kilometres of unpaved road from the Klondike Highway near Dawson City in the Yukon to Inuvik in the Northwest Territories.

We are gearing up. At the outdoor equipment store in North Vancouver, I ask the young man to help me find a balaclava. He's helpful and mildly interested, probably thinking I'm going to walk the West Vancouver seawall in winter. I tell him I need it for temperatures which could reach minus 40. I have his attention now.

"Where are you going?"

"We're driving the Dempster Highway — in March."

"Wow, that's awesome!" He's with me now. The Dempster has a reputation for being one of Canada's most dangerous roads, a year-round thrill ride from which no windshield emerges unscathed.

He takes great time and care with me then, interested in the trip, glad that I'm preparing properly. He finds me a neoprene balaclava, a smooth black hood with just an eye opening. I try it on at his insistence, and it feels good.

"Would you like to see it in the mirror?" he asks.

"No," I say, "no." I've long passed the point where looking in the mirror delivers any rewards.

"Come on, come and see it in the mirror," he says as he walks across the store, waving at me to come with him.

I follow him to the mirror, turn and look.

"You see," he says, "you look like a ninja warrior!" His words make my spirits soar. I'm turning seventy and I'm a ninja warrior.

"Have a great adventure," he says. "You'll come back changed."

I'm already changed. His words have changed me, made me remember who I was — who I am.

Before we leave Vancouver I proudly go over my gear list with my son-in-law, a search and rescue specialist. "My boots, coats, and gloves are rated for minus 50, we have extra food and water, blankets …"

"How will you communicate?" he asks. "You can have the best gear in the world, but if there's an accident and no one knows you need help, your gear isn't going to save you." I call Whitehorse that day and rent a satellite phone.

On a cool Vancouver morning we lift off out of YVR, up and away across the Coast Mountains and north, bound for White-horse. Air North is genuinely 'Yukon's Airline', one hundred percent owned by Yukoners, including the Vuntut Gwich'in First Nation. People call to each other up and down the aisles. It feels like a community gathering. Snatches of conversation show us how far we are from Vancouver's urban buzz. *How's the Fortymile caribou hunt? Is the ice road to Aklavik still solid? Did your* *mother get down from Old Crow?* The flight attendants come round with warm, homemade chocolate chip cookies. Regulars have been expecting these, and enthusiasm surges through the cabin.

For a while we keep the coast on our port wing, but then we curve towards BC's interior. There are always mountains, snow-capped, getting higher and steeper; frozen lakes and glaciers, ancient rivers like white snakes coiling round on themselves and back again. About two hours into the flight we see a vast Pacific fjord stretching out, a wild, splintered coast, with inlets running far from the sea into the interior of Alaska and the Yukon. Below us, the White Pass, the Chilkoot Trail, the Klondike Highway—names burned into the Canadian imagination. Gold!

The wing dips low and we take a wide, deep turn along the Yukon River, a ribbon of ice winding through Whitehorse. On the riverbank, we can see the great paddle-wheeler S.S. *Klondike*, stranded and silent, which once carried dreams of gold to Dawson City. On the escarpment above the town, the runways and terminals of Erik Nielsen Airport line up with us and we touch down. There's a buzz of excitement. It feels like a homecoming.

Whitehorse is a melting pot of cultural, artistic, and culinary experiences, with a pervasive sense of history, from the rich ancient culture of the Yukon's First Nations to the legendary artefacts of the Klondike gold rush. There's art on every corner, its themes deeply connected to the land and its history, from *The Box of Light* drawn from Tlingit legend to *The Prospector and his Dog* and the bronze of Angela Sidney, Tagish storyteller. There are busts of Pierre Berton, Jack London, and Robert Service, and the magical *Raven House*, a light, airy sculpture you can walk inside. There's the spectacular Kwanlin Dün Cultural Centre, museums to explore, rivers and lakes to paddle, trails to walk. Best of all, there are people who'll always stop to greet a stranger.

Whitehorse is the north — and it feels like it, but we are going onward and upward. Our destination is the Arctic Ocean.

A friend who lives in Whitehorse is going with us — safety in numbers, especially on the Dempster. We leave Whitehorse in tandem, our friend in his rented black Chevy Suburban and us in our white one. We figure that if we get lost in the snow, rescuers will at least see him. We have walkie-talkies with a range of up to 30 kilometres and, of course, our satellite phone.

The first leg of our drive is to Dawson City, about 530 km away. Our first break is at Braeburn, the classic truck stop between Whitehorse and Dawson and an official checkpoint for the Yukon Quest, the international sled dog race along a 1600 km wilderness trail between Fairbanks, Alaska, and Whitehorse.

This place hasn't changed for decades. The walls are covered with team times, Quest posters, photos of famous dogs and their mushers. In the corner, an older man with a long white beard is sitting at a table with his coffee in a Styrofoam mug. He's seen our polar bear licence plates and asks where we're going. We tell him we're heading to Inuvik. "Inuvik," he says. "There's a round church there. You know why it's round? So the devil can't hide in the corners." An odd, unsettling thought, the devil trying to hide in a church. We take a seat and help ourselves to coffee and Coffee-Mate, and there on the counter, beside the coffee-pot, are the biggest cinnamon buns we've ever seen, as big as dinner plates and six inches high. We have to get one. We have a bite or two each, but it's still massive, so we take it with us. If we get stuck on the Dempster, it will keep the three of us alive for days.

By the time we reach Dawson City, it's been snowing and thawing and the roads are piled with slush. Just one night there for us, at the Dawson Hotel (with the obligatory Sourtoe Cocktail) and we're away again. The Dempster turn-off is forty kilometres back along the Klondike. The sign says *Highway 5 North, Fort McPherson and Inuvik.* Fort McPherson and Inuvik are 546 and 737 kilometres away respectively, above the Arctic Circle. There is nothing but wilderness for us now, until the solitary Eagle Plains Hotel at kilometre 369.

We stop to take 'before' photos of ourselves and our vehicles. *You'll come back changed.*

There's a jumble of road signs at the entrance to the road. The most exciting is the big wooden Yukon Government Dempster Highway interpretive sign, with maps, pictures, and travel cautions on its four-square posts, all of it capped by a painted blue arc, which we'll come to recognize as we travel on. But there are other signs too: *One-lane bridge, 30 km speed limit* (if you're lucky; it's March). *There are no emergency road services on the Yukon section of the Dempster Highway — drive with care.*

We cross a wooden bridge, and excitement spills over. We're driving the Dempster! One minute later, another sign stops us short. *Peel River Crossing NWT km 539 Dempster Highway. For more information contact …* Slapped across it, in huge capital letters, is the word *CLOSED.* The Peel River Crossing is the ice bridge over the only route to the Arctic from here. We're shocked that it's closed. It's far too early for the ice to be breaking up. Can our Dempster adventure really be ending at kilometre one? We talk about risking it, but 500 kilometres of wilderness is too big a risk, so we phone the Northwest Territories information number on the sign. There is only a very old message and no information, so we call the Eagle Plains Hotel, the only stopping place in 5 0 0 kilometres of wilderness. A woman answers. "The ice crossings are good," she says. "We have people who've just come across. Ignore that sign—they haven't changed it since last October." We breathe again, and on we go.

The road is good, not the white-knuckle driving we'd feared, and it's a welcome surprise. There's snow, but enough gravel for traction. The weather is clear, visibility's high, the air is crisp and cold, and we can see to the far horizons. By the time we reach Tombstone National Park at kilometre 7 1, we are overwhelmed by the sheer vastness of the expanses and the waves of colour, even in winter: blue, grey, purple, green, brown, black. The scale is almost more than we can take in. Away, far away from anything we can call familiar, is a primaeval landscape of wide, ancient plains and alluvial valleys guarded by jagged mountains, endless white, with turquoise-blue ice on the lakes and rivers. We are out of place here. Small. Awestruck.

There's something deeply fulfilling about travelling in our own country. It's the same thrill of adventure and exploration we feel when we travel outside our borders but there's an underlying sense of home, of recognition. In the immense and overwhelming north in particular, we need to immerse ourselves in this sense of belonging, to sink in.

We stop to take photos and realize we're taking a lot of close-ups. Ice, pine needles, berries, rocks, snow. It's a scale we can grasp.

Meanwhile, The highway stretches far ahead of us, curving away across soft white hills and into the mountains on the way to the Arctic Circle. From 1 9 0 4 to 1 9 2 1, the Northwest Mounted Police trekked this unforgiving land on annual patrols from Dawson to Fort McPherson, a route of nearly 1 0 0 0 kilometres, which took a hard month's travelling. There would be no road for another sixty years. One of these men was Corporal William John Dempster, thought to be the best trail man in the Yukon. For several years he led the winter patrols, marking trails and building supply caches and shelters. In 1917 he was asked to find a route from the Porcupine River to Dawson, and with the help of First Nations people, he found a way through the uncharted Ogilvie Mountains. Dempster died in 1964 at the age of eighty-eight, but shortly before his death, he was told that the highway being constructed from Dawson to Inuvik would be named in his honour.

There are not many trees beside us now, and those that survive are thin, with all the growth on the top, as if all they can do in this deep cold is send their strength to the highest needles so they'll catch the last rays of the winter sun. We reach a crest, and a huge valley stretches out below us: Eagle Plains. Somewhere down there is a small hotel, waiting for us with a room and a hot meal. We see the flags first, Canadian flags and the flag of the Yukon, a shock of bright colour across the winter palette of the Dempster.

Eagle Plains Hotel — the place, the legend — spreads long and low beside a significant length of road, with lodging, gas, highway maintenance, truck stop, emergency services, and everything to keep a traveller safe, warm, happy, and prepared. An oasis in the wilderness. It's rustic, one-story, only 35 kilometres from the Arctic Circle. It fits in. The road is solid ice here. We are 369 kilometres up the Dempster.

We get inside, away from the wind and freezing cold, and head to the heart of the place: the bar. There are antlers, pelts, and snowshoes on the walls and ceiling, stuffed wild animals in friezes around the room. We sit next to a group of caribou standing in plastic tropical ferns. The bar is filled with travellers and long-distance truckers, and all the talk is about 'going to the Circle' and 'going over the top' (to the Northwest Territories). A high-wind warning has come up, especially dangerous in hurricane alley, a few kilometres to the north of Eagle Plains. The winds can be deadly up here.

After dinner we sit by the fire, nursing our beers. A trucker wanders over. "Where're you guys staying tonight?" he asks.

"Here."

"Good. Don't go up hurricane alley. Winds are gusting to 130 km. Even the big rigs are getting blown around. Don't leave tomorrow until the winds die down."

He tells us that last night, a big rig fishtailed south of here and blocked the highway all night. There were several cars stuck behind it, including a family with small children. Everyone made it through until morning, but it's a stark reminder that on this highway, anything can happen.

In the morning the wind has died down, and we head for the Arctic Circle, stopping in the numbing cold to take photos by the big sign. I take off my gloves for a moment to click the shutter, and it takes me a long, long time to get my hands warm again. First Arctic lesson learned.

The coldest stopping place by far is the border between the Yukon and the Northwest Territories. It's minus 30 and blowing, and I put on my balaclava. Arctic ninja warrior. The landscape changes as we drive into the Territories. Rolling hills like melted marshmallow ripple away into the distance. There is no vegetation here, just the topography with all its shapes and contours, empty except for us and a few snow buntings. At kilometre 5 3 9 from the Klondike Highway junction, we reach the Peel River ice crossing. It's not very wide and, with relief, we see that it's open. The snow on the river has been ploughed to make a road. We drive slowly, trying to be mindful of it all in the moment, aware of the ice under our wheels. One ice bridge down, one to go, and we drive up the riverbank and on to the Dene settlement of Fort McPherson, the first town we've seen in nearly 6 0 0 kilometres. The final resting place of the Lost Patrol.

On December 21, 1910, four members of the Northwest Mounted Police, led by Inspector Francis Joseph Fitzgerald, set out from Fort McPherson to travel to Dawson City. They left with fifteen dogs, three sleds, and enough food for thirty days. By January 1 2, 1 9 1 1, the patrol was lost with few rations remaining. The last entry in Inspector Fitzgerald's diary was February 5: "My last hope is gone …" When a relief patrol found them on March 2 1, there was no one left alive. They're buried in Fort McPherson in the small, snow-deep cemetery, and their names have passed into legend. The Lost Patrol. We walk around their graves, thinking of them—small, lost, and powerless against this immense wilderness and this merciless cold.

After Fort McPherson, our mood changes from awe to anticipation. We crest a hill, and far below us is the Mackenzie River Delta, a wide sweep of frozen river banked by high cliffs. It looks like the sea. We're heading down and into my dream on a Vancouver night, weeks ago — the Mackenzie River ice crossing.

The ice road is wide enough for two big trucks to pass with room to spare. This crossing takes much longer than the Peel. The ice is blue under our wheels. I'm holding my breath, but the distance is too far, and halfway across I breathe in the deep mystery of crossing the ice, as humans have done for thousands of years. On the far bank, the ferry is locked in by winter, waiting for spring. We drive past it, up to the road and on. *Done.* We're flying home from Inuvik so will not pass this way again. The ice bridges are done, my dream fears conquered.

I do not know yet that there's a 2 0 0-kilometre ice road ahead of us on this journey.

Inuvik lies in the Taiga Plains, south of the tree line that marks the beginning of Arctic tundra. In the heart of the Mackenzie Delta, Inuvik is on the traditional land of the Inuvialuit, Gwich'in, and Métis people. It's a young town, built in the 1 9 5 0 s and '6 0 s as a replacement administrative centre for the town of Aklavik, 1 0 0 kilometres away in the west of the Mackenzie Delta on the Peel Channel. Aklavik was subject to severe annual flooding and the riverbanks were being washed away, taking parts of the community with them. Many people moved to Inuvik, but a core group, unwilling to give up history and heritage, stayed. The community survived.

The ice road to Aklavik is calling — 2 0 0 kilometres there and back across the Mackenzie Delta, on river ice the whole way. We know the risks, but we go of course, and it's very different from the river crossings we've done before. This time we're on ice for hours, and we have to find a new way to think about it to hold back primal fear. Even my daunting Vancouver dream did not conjure the magnitude and menace of this. At the beginning the riverbanks are only a car length away, and we joke about how we could make it if we went through the ice. Then the delta sprawls out, and the river banks are so far away on the horizon that we can't see the edge. We stop talking.

There are no landmarks. People wayfind here by giving places names that describe them: the place where the sweet blueberries are, the place where he got his first seal, the small hill coloured green at sunset. This is a recognition of absolute common ground, of territory so familiar that even one small hill coloured green is distinct and known. Our ice road is blue and green with huge cracks and deep ruts, dazzling in the sun. Halfway to Aklavik, we get out to stand on the road and take pictures of our boots with the clear ice dropping away beneath them. We imagine that we can see the river flowing, but it is locked away.

In Aklavik, we drive up the riverbank into a town that seems deserted, hunkered down against the bitter cold. About 6 0 0 Gwich'in and Inuvialuit people make their living here, trapping and fishing. Almost every house has a snowmobile; some have boats pulled up, covered with snow, ice-locked until spring. Old log cabins mix easily with new wooden houses. As we drive through empty streets back to the Mackenzie River, we come across a group of kids happily pulling a sled in defiance of sub-zero, testament to Aklavik's town motto: 'Never Say Die'. We wave goodbye. We have 1 0 0 kilometres of ice road to cover on the way back to Inuvik, with a very special place to stop halfway there.

A friend of our fellow traveller has invited us to spend the evening sharing a campfire, caribou stew, and bannock in the traditional village he builds every year to offer the experience of sleeping in an igloo and hearing about the ancient ways. When we see his truck on the side of the river, we park next to it and head into the bush on foot, across a frozen lake. In the distance we see the igloos clustered like blue glass bubbles in the setting sun.

As night falls, we sit on beaver pelts on the floor of the biggest igloo, eating muktuk and listening to stories of the people who once lived like this, the Inuvialuit and the Gwich'in.

Light comes through the ice walls, sunset filtered and frosted like gold dust, and after dark there's a glow beneath the ice floor. When we crawl out of the igloo, there's a bright moon in the sky, and we don't turn on our headlamps.

As the three of us walk back to the ice road, we hear owls call to each other from the trees. There are tracks in the snow on top of the tracks we made coming in. Not human. Large paw prints. We hurry to our vehicle and drive back to Inuvik with the ice road glistening in the moonlight.

On a new road piled high with snow, we head for Tuktoyaktuk, 138 kilometres away. Tuk stands at the bright, brilliant edge of the Arctic Ocean. Long before Franklin searched for the Northwest Passage, the Inuvialuit people here lived, hunted, fished and profoundly understood their world. I feel small and humble, but connected to everything as seamlessly as the white of the snow meeting the white of the ice-bound sea. We take pictures of each other by the big blue Arctic Ocean sign to prove to others — and to ourselves — that we've made it. The ice rafts up to the horizon, and it's colder than I've ever felt. We are animals at the edge of the ice.

The next day we are outbound, southbound for Whitehorse on an Air North ATR 42 — part cargo, part passenger plane. As we sit in our seats under the wings, ready for take-off, I can't hold back the tears at the loss of all of this. It's visceral, deeply personal.

We lift off from the landscape of the first days of the world, up and slowly away. Below us are all the things that make up the history of this land, trapped in ice: mammoth tusks, the Lost Patrol, the art and artefacts of First People who came this way 14,000 years ago. Below us, the frozen, fractured Arctic Ocean, the tundra, a thousand lakes, sinuous rivers.

In the distance, away on the horizon, the Richardson Mountains carve the boundary between the Northwest Territories and the Yukon. Dominating the landscape, the mighty Mackenzie River threads white seams across the alluvial plain like a great tapestry. Below us are Inuvik, Tuktoyaktuk, and Aklavik, with its formidable ice road etching a blue line across the Delta. We can see the jagged mountain glaciers of Tombstone. Somewhere down there is Eagle Plains.

And from the very beginning of the flight we see the road. We climb higher and higher and we can still see it, the reason for our Arctic journey, the extraordinary Dempster Highway, tracing an ancient human path through the stark and endless beauty of the north. I am forever changed.

THE RAVEN SHORT STORY CONTEST

THE 2023 RAVEN SHORT STORY CONTEST

The 2023 Raven Short Story Contest gave us another year of wonderfully crafted, challenging stories. A hearty thank-you to all who submitted. You made this crop of Ravens especially difficult to narrow down. Fortunately, our talented final judge, Kelly Robson, was up to the task of choosing our winner. Kelly praised all eleven of the shortlisted stories as *"very accomplished, with vivid prose and surprising, original imaginative leaps. Congratulations to all!"*

WINNER: **'Neverender' by Krista Jane May**

UNRANKED RUNNERS-UP: **'Flehmen Grimace' by EC Dorgan**, and **'Watercolours' by EC Dorgan**

And congratulations to the authors who made the 2023 Raven Shortlist:

EC Dorgan for 'Flehmen Grimace'
EC Dorgan for 'Watercolours'
Jonathan Sean Lyster for 'Liar's Leap'
Kevin Sandefur for 'Daughters of the Earth and Sky'
Krista Jane May for 'Neverender'
Leslie Wibberley for 'See the Pretty Girl'
Lisa Jones for 'The Loom'
Lisa Seaman for 'The Projectionist'

Mitchell Toews for 'The Invisible Light'
Robert Runté for 'Summoning Demons'
Tyner Gillies for 'It's Okay To Dance'

Manitoba born and raised, **Krista Jane May** *currently resides in rural Saskatchewan after years on both east and west coasts. Her work can be found in such journals as* Grain, The Antigonish Review, CommuterLit, *and* The Garfield Lake Review. *Her story 'Fate of Chickens' appeared in* Pulp Literature *Issue 33. She took second place in the 2019 Lorian Hemingway Short Story Competition, and was longlisted for the 2021 CBC Short Story Prize. This is her first time in first place.*

*N*EVERENDER

BY KRISTA JANE MAY

The wind, the wind, the wind blows high, toss——

"Hey! Lorena! If you're not doing anything, how about a fresh pot of coffee?"

What William——shouting from behind the closed door of his study——is really saying is: *Stop what you're doing. It's not important like what I'm doing and I want coffee. Now. Make some.*

He's not entirely wrong. Lorena is, after all, merely standing in the bathroom, pondering the oak-framed portrait above the sink. She's looking closely. Brown spots on cheeks, creases around mouth, puffiness surrounding dull, weary eyes. Loose skin at the neck drapes in folds that disappear into a cavern of a throat; it looks as if one could crawl in there and never find one's way out. How is it possible, she wonders, that a woman can look this way on the outside yet inside feel like a hapless, half-grown child? Surely a face so portrayed is worthy of one who has gained — if not exactly admiration — a place of respect, something she's certain the woman who displays it has not. But the reflected lines don't lie: this woman has clearly lived the number of years required to obtain such spectacular results. Yet it surprises — sometimes shocks — her whenever she studies this face. She believes the woman who wears it hasn't earned one bit of it.

Tossing Lor-e-na through the sky —

But *coffee*. Right. She turns to leave the bathroom, then stops.

She'd allowed it to happen, of course. She won't cry about it, and she'd be ashamed to share her thoughts with even her closest of friends who, in any case, have dwindled to rather few. She already knows what those two or three would say, if presented with such an unsavoury task: *Nonsense! You look fantastic!* (she doesn't), *You've accomplished many great things!* (she hasn't), or *You're definitely no doormat!* (she is). Nor would she seek professional solace. Why pay for the same lies — albeit tied up with a pretty ribbon around an expensive, mind-numbing prescription — that her friends would offer free? Anyway, who could be a better authority on her, other than herself? She can do her own analysis, go back to the beginning, use that thoughtless, impractical, but oh-so-costly gift of hindsight. Point out — to and by her very own self — exactly where she'd gone wrong.

"First of all, you should never have allowed yourself to be a neverender."

That far back? She's cruel. Lorena glares resentfully at the old bitch, who returns her hateful gaze. They give each other the finger.

Neverender, NE-ver-EN-der … It was the invariable, shrieking sing-song response of the venerated ones, those schoolgirls who called the shots on the skipping pavement at recess if you somehow managed the courage to ask if you could join in. The term was, technically, 'ever-ender' meaning that those glowing girls — who had it all figured out so young — would condescend to let you clutch the purple-and-orange-striped handle of someone's deluxe skipping rope and, like a machine precise in its rhythms, turn it — over and over — while they jumped. You were allowed to participate in the accompanying chant, particularly those jingles conjuring the skipper's winning the undying love of a certain boy, joyfully clueless, off somewhere kicking a soccer ball.

She can play acCORdion, one two THREE! Tell me, TELL me, WHO is HE? Wah-un, two-oo, THREE!

You'd then have to sing the alphabet whilst turning the rope *pepper* — or very fast — making sure not to trip up the jumper until she reached the desired letter, say *R* for Ricky, at which point she'd willingly trip herself up, confirming Ricky as her true love. You dared not admit a crush on Ricky yourself.

She wonders if Caroline Boyer was a neverender as a child. Caroline Boyer is the freelance author of too many CBC lifestyle articles, cringe-worthy ramblings Lorena has vowed never to read again. But there are times — such as this morning — when some masochistic shadow strangles her better judgement. Caroline is exactly Lorena's age, and today's article (in the once stately national broadcaster turned online tabloid) elaborates on her dawning comprehension that, at fifty-seven, she is no longer noticed when she goes about her daily business of, say, sipping a latte in an upscale bistro or scrolling messages whilst lounging on a bench in the exchange district's food cart zone, an area frequented by trendy young lawyers and well-coiffed junior financiers. Apparently, throughout Caroline's prolonged youth, she'd received daily male attention, some of it enjoyably flirtatious, though most (she not-quite-convincingly stresses) despicably suggestive if not altogether aggressive. In any case, it all affirms that she was once a highly desirable woman. And now she is suddenly not. Ms Boyer fails to conclude, despite the generous word count allotted to her, whether her new invisible status is to be lamented or celebrated. There is an accompanying photo of the author: attractive (despite a rather manic light in the heavily made-up eyes), with a wide blinding smile, unnaturally natural-looking hair, and—most appalling—not a wrinkle, not a hint of saggy skin. Whether image or woman (or both) have been extensively tampered with is of no consequence to Lorena, who vows again to avoid such soul-sapping surfing. Never an ever-ender, she decides: Caroline Boyer is a dedicated, lifelong jumper.

A-B-Cee-D-E-F-Gee ... If you messed up—it was always a neverender's fault—the skipper got another chance, and another, until the results were triumphantly achieved and the spotlight relinquished to the next most popular girl. In fair skipping, the finished jumper takes an end, but in Lorena's young world, only the Carolines jumped; you understood that, once enslaved, only the bell could free you. But there was something tantalizing about that candy-like rope handle that always drew her, something almost as intriguing as the liquorice allsorts her mother—on special occasions—let her father keep in a fragile Edwardian porcelain bowl. Almost like if you bit into that soft rubber, it would taste like one of those occasionally allowed, dream-coloured, family heirloom-worthy sweets.

... H-I-Jay-K-L—

"Lorena! Where the hell *are* you?" Lorena startles, but reaches for the inner doorknob and quietly pulls the slightly open bathroom door closed. It's a small house; she hears his door open, hears the squeaking resistance of wary floorboards as William strides towards the kitchen, huffs exaggeratedly, then heads back to his study, not *quite* slamming the door behind him. It's her second warning. She glances again at the pitiless woman in the mirror, then turns away, sits down on the closed toilet seat and pulls up the hem of her cotton skirt. Fifty years, and the scar on her knee is still red.

She hadn't been able to resist. Bored with turning the rope, mesmerized by the irresistible striped neon, she'd brought the rubber handle to her mouth, licked it. She remembers more the inexplicable surprise at finding no sugary sweetness there than she does the violent shove to the pavement, which was always strewn with rough gravel from the nearby swing pits. She'd scraped her knee so badly that she'd been carried by an alerted teacher to the nurse's station. But, though it hurt, her crying had more to do with her fear of bloodying her new hot-pink knee socks, worn for the first time that sunny spring day with her favourite outfit: a bright, baby elephant-patterned sundress with matching ruffled underpants, one of those special outfits you put on with a feeling that today was to be a momentous day. In Mrs Cartwright's arms, she had pushed her sock further and further towards her ankle as the gushing river of blood relentlessly pursued the ribbed elastic cuff. Likely the nylon socks had been easy enough for her mother to wash or inexpensive enough to replace, but at six, so afraid had she been of ruining them that the throbbing pain of the pebble-encrusted wound was moot. She had not tattled, had insisted the incident had been an accident. Clumsy her.

M-En-O-Pee—

"Goddamn it, Lorena, do I have to make the coffee myself?"

Now is the time to rush out, grab the kettle, apologize to William for taking so long in the bathroom: bit of a tummy ache, sorry. She stands but remains where she is, studies again the woman over the sink. She appears to have softened, seems a little gentler now in her tone:

"Look, Caroline Boyer hasn't considered something vital. While she insists she's relieved to be free of certain unwanted attentions, she undeniably regrets losing the admiration of others. But the appealing ones—the bistro cutie behind the milk steamer, the radical clerk in the bookstore—are not her contemporaries. The young men of her day—of *our* day—are gone; like us, they've ceased to be young. And wouldn't it be horrifying if they *hadn't* changed? Imagine a distinguished-looking sixty-year-old man in a well-tailored suit suddenly making catcalls. Anyone would be appalled."

Lorena nods: the woman makes sense. When Caroline Boyer was twenty, she would not have been ogling grandfathers, but now—admittedly a grandmother herself—she wishes for the attention of the attractive young men. It's a double standard, but then, jumpers are greedy. *Oh, Caroline. Could it be* you *who is doing the ignoring? Probably you are admired still, but quietly, perhaps by some worthy soul with a craggy face. And if not, so what?* Lorena smiles at the oak-framed woman, who smiles approvingly back. She *has* changed. Is it a stretch to think she looks almost … *pretty?* Probably, but she'll settle for resolved.

"Fuck!" William seems to have spilled coffee beans all over the floor, but Lorena resists the instinct to rush out and start cleaning up the mess. Eventually she hears the grinder going, the sound of his pacing as he waits for the kettle to boil.

Q-R-Ess-T-U-Vee-W—

William. Even William must have done his share of looking as a young man, though Lorena has a hard time picturing him leering or growling or making suggestive moves. They'd been a little older when they'd met, a bit mature. But they'd both had their youth; he had to have spent his … *somehow.* Funny she'd never given it much thought. Now, every day, he shuts himself in his study, writes his important papers.

Tee-U-V … DOUBLE You—

"Lorena?"

William is rapping on the bathroom door. She quickly lowers herself to the toilet seat.

"Lorena!" He's pounding now. She feigns an unwell look as he eases open the unlocked door.

"Jesus. I've been calling, you didn't answer … Hey, are you okay?"

She is astounded by his sudden softness, the unfamiliar gentle tone.

"I—I'm fine. I was just feeling a little off, but I'm better now." It's not a lie.

"Okay." He hesitates. "Well, I've made coffee if you're up to it. Not as good as yours, but …" He shrugs, surprises her with a hint of that devastating smile she'd almost forgotten he possessed.

"Thank you," she says. "I'll just be a minute."

Not long after the playground episode, Lorena had asked for a skipping rope of her own. Her parents had—reluctantly, she recalls—indulged her wish, and on her seventh birthday, she'd received an exquisite long rope in turquoise and pink, her favourite colours. It hadn't worked. Even with her beautiful new rope, those girls still wanted her, endlessly, to turn for *them*.

Lorena rises, smooths down her skirt. The woman over the sink beckons as she tries to pass her by, whispers so that William, in the kitchen, can't hear.

"You'd forgotten, hadn't you? What you learned so long ago."

Lorena stops and faces her head on.

"All you've *ever* had to do is drop your end of the rope."

The woman's smile briefly flickers childhood's triumph as she watches Lorena remember. *Of course.* Lorena stares in awe at this confident, oak-framed face. She's right: Lorena had, eventually, left the Carolines behind. She'd learned to roll the extra lengths of her own lovely rope securely around her wrists so she could jump to her heart's content, all on her own. She heads for the kitchen. The coffee William made smells delicious.

PULP Literature

The Bumblebee
Flash Fiction Contest
Deadline: 15 February
Prize $300

The Magpie Award for Poetry
Deadline: 15 April
Prize $500

The Hummingbird Flash Fiction Prize
Deadline: 15 June
Prize $300

The Raven Short Story Contest
Deadline: 15 October
Prize $300

The Kingfisher Poetry Prize
Deadline: 15 November
Prize $300

Enter today:
pulpliterature.com/contests

EC Dorgan writes dark fiction and monster stories on Treaty 6 territory near Edmonton, Canada. She has stories published and/or forthcoming in Augur, The Ex-Puritan, *and* Metaphorosis. *Her story 'Moon Eater' appeared in* Pulp Literature *Issue 41. She is a member of the Métis Nation of Alberta.*

Flehmen Grimace

by EC Dorgan

He's there and then he isn't, and sometimes I'm not sure if he's a buffalo or something older. This is oil country. Dinosaurs are in our bones. The calcium and phosphorous lining our skulls comes from the spines of Tyrannosaurus baptized in holy black crude.

This buffalo, he watches me. Flicking his tail and chewing scrubby weeds. He's dark brown, and his beard is so long it brushes the ground.

At first, I wondered what he was doing in my backyard. I live in the city centre. The buffalo live farther east, under the shadow of refineries.

There's something else about this buffalo. I can see the grass and the back shed right through him.

The first time I see him, I mean really see him, he's standing there, nostrils flaring, breathing puffs of air in the frigid late spring day. He must be two thousand pounds. I lift my upper lip but don't smell a thing. I inhale, and accidentally breathe in ghost.

There's a piece of that ghost that sticks in me. It makes me want to thunder down the prairie. I'm not made for it. My stomach turns, and I barely make it to the toilet bowl. My vomit is black crude.

Spring turns to summer. One morning I come outside to find my grass replaced by dirt. And the hollow of a beast in the ground. Now I know buffalo ghosts have mud baths, too.

His lashes are long and his tail wags at ghost sandflies. One day I lift my upper lip and breathe as though my vomero-nasal organ isn't vestigial. As though humans can read pheromones like buffalo. But it's the ghost I breathed, not the roof of my mouth, that translates for me: the buffalo wants its bones back.

At first, I don't know what that has to do with me. Then I remember the crude, the toilet. I still have some of that calcium-phosphorus breath stuck inside of me.

The buffalo looms in the yard and waits. After a week, an idea. I can't give it bones, but I have teeth.

One day I wait for him. I have a plan. Pliers to pull, cheesecloth for blood. Twine in case I lose my nerve. When the buffalo appears in my yard, I stand in the window facing it. The pliers are cold and metallic. I touch them to my tooth and shudder.

The buffalo watches.

I tell him. "I'm giving you teeth."

He keeps chewing.

I open my mouth and position the pliers. The metal rings through my fillings to my spine and the base of my skull. I want to shake. I close the pliers around my molar and tighten. There's a rush of cold pressure. All my real and imagined fillings flash, and blue lightning runs up and down my spine. I pull out the pliers in a rush and spit out metallic saliva.

The buffalo doesn't blink.

I put the pliers down on the windowsill. My molar throbs. I take the twine and fit my thumb into my mouth. It's hard to tie it around my molar. My fingernails brush my gums and my palate. I finally tie it tight. The pressure makes my jaw smart.

The buffalo stops chewing. It occurs to me I should have tied the other end first.

I tell the ghost, "Hold still."

The twine makes my enunciation funny.

The buffalo stares.

It's not so easy to tie a string around a transparent tail, but I manage.

I take two steps back. The buffalo lifts his lip and makes a grimace. Something rumbles underground, and we both look down. The earth quiets. The buffalo and I meet eyes. We both know there are things that are older. We wait for the Tyrannosaurus to return to its slumber.

Perhaps I should have thought this through. When I was a child and we'd just moved to this oil city ringed by buffalo and refineries, my dentist pulled out my baby molar and said it would feel like nothing. It didn't.

The buffalo tilts its head at me. Its eyes are so big I can see my reflection. And the twine connecting us. I take a step to the buffalo to loosen the knot. The buffalo lifts its upper lip, and I know that vomero-nasal organ is working. I freeze. The buffalo runs.

It doesn't feel like nothing. The pain arches into my palate and through my jaws; it makes my eardrums ring and my spine shudder. It ripples into the earth from the base of my skull to my heels dug deep. I reach out for the cheesecloth and press it against my bleeding mouth. Feel my tongue over the empty, wet space.

I take the cheesecloth out of my mouth. It's black with crude. I drop to my knees on the earth and lift my lip. Can't smell a thing with my absent organ. I bend over and press my mouth into the earth. It tastes like metal and petroleum. I lift my lip and take it in. I don't know if it's the piece of that ghost that's still in me, or maybe the piece of me in that buffaloed molar, but something wakes.

I blink, and I'm standing in a backyard, or in the ghost of one. A buffalo is watching me from a window. It has a pair of pliers in its mouth and a ball of twine. The oily hollow in my jaw pangs, and I grimace.

I see myself reflected in its eyes. How the buffalo sees the grass and the shed behind me. I reach for my hollowed jaw and my hand goes right through me.

The buffalo chews scrubby weeds with its new molar. It lifts its lip and makes a grimace, then breathes me in.

Watercolours

by EC Dorgan

Tonight we're roasting marshmallows under a meat sky; if we hold our straightened clothes-hangers at the right angle, the flesh will impale itself onto the metal and stain the caramelized marshmallow a lusty pink.

If my son were here, he'd be recording. He's smart to find his way in the New Economy. I have a neighbour who makes their living walking along the white picket fence, mouth open to the sky, filming, catching meat.

It's only my wife I wonder about. She's always frowning at the sky with wet eyes.

Before the New Economy, she painted watercolours. Now she's renounced art. She doesn't like the new meat sunsets, and that's why it's just me and my daughter with our marshmallows. My wife won't go outside when it meat-rains. Last winter, during the meat-blizzard, she locked herself in the basement and made us professionally clean the windows before opening the curtains.

A hunk of flesh impales itself on my clothes-hanger, and the juices splatter on my cheek. I wipe my face. The meat stains my marshmallow. My daughter takes it.

She's just like me. Embracing the New Economic Order. She's already taking tourists meat-fishing in the sky using our old lawn-mower tractor and a roll of yarn.

There's only one marshmallow left when my wife comes out of the house, wearing gloves and holding an umbrella.

I call to her, "Will you paint us?"

Her face falls, and my daughter gives me one of those killer teen looks. She drops her metal wire, and her marshmallow falls onto the blue tarp where we collect meat. She walks to her mother and they go inside.

A hunk of meat falls on my cheek. I tilt my head up to the sky and get the next one in my eye. There's a bone in it, a femur or a pelvis. It knocks me clean unconscious.

And just like that, I'm twenty-seven again. I have hair. My belly's flat. When I look out the window, the sky is blue. We're just married. Not even thinking about kids. My wife is still painting.

We thought smartphones were a thing, but they're nothing compared to this new invention. The youth call it 'fire'. It is the new fire. The iFeed app. The latest AI-fuelled ingenuity. A solution to world hunger. A means of production with no cost or waste.

I was a late adopter. It dropped on the iStore on a Monday, and I waited a week to download it. My wife downloaded it on the third day, but she deleted it two days later. Deleted all her data, too.

It's our anniversary, and she makes striploin. We eat it rare on a red tablecloth with full-bodied Shiraz that drips down our chins and stinky candles that melt on the table. We turn off our phones, though it almost kills us.

My wife takes my hand and looks me in the eyes and says, "Stay real."

The next morning, she paints me at the table with the wine. She says it's my anniversary gift. At work I get another anniversary gift—a terse email from my boss saying I'm being terminated. This, after I've used my savings and taken a giant mortgage to finance our dream house …

They say the iFeed is the New Economy. I download the app that same day. My wife flushes her watercolours down the toilet the day after.

When I open my eyes, I have the thought that I'm face down on the table cloth. But I'm on my back. I'm facing the red sky. My eye hurts. I touch it and feel blood, but it's not mine, it's fallen flesh.

I reach into my shirt pocket and pull out my phone. Open my iFeed app, though I don't really need to. Now that it's uploaded to the sky, the phone is more for convenience, or habit.

I should get moving. There are a hundred opportunities in the New Economy that I could be capitalizing on. I could livestream my marshmallow-roasting and make money right from this tarp.

I sit up and look back at the house I paid off thanks to the New Economy. A hunk of flesh lands on my shin. I pick it up and chew it.

When I first met my wife, she painted me with watercolours in a field of wild roses in autumn. The earth was crimson from the dying stems and the sky was blue. Now the sky is red and the ground is blue from the tarp.

I used to think buying a house was the most important thing. Funny how life turns things round. I should be grateful to be living in this time of opportunity. I look out at the fire pit, the house. One day, my kids will inherit this.

I want them to be proud of me. I hold up my phone and pick up my clothes-hanger. Figure it's never too late to up-skill. I hit record, then watch the viewers increase. A hunk of meat falls on the wire and I take a bite. Little dollars light up on my FeedBank, and I get the hundred-dollar-bill chime. It gives me a thrill.

Then I see my wife standing beside the house with her umbrella. She dabs a handkerchief at her eyes. She threw out her phone years ago.

I keep my mouth smiling. Try to keep my eyes fixed on that image in the viewfinder — me and my giant house, reaping the good fortune of the New Economy.

But inside, a different feeling. My gut rocks. Reeling from something I've lost.

The next thing I know, I'm down. Grasping for that crimson tablecloth, for my wife's hand, not finding it. Trying to breathe something other than meat.

I can't see my wife's face under the umbrella. My smile becomes a grimace.

I lift my head. My wife turns her back. Then I'm choking and drowning in watercolour.

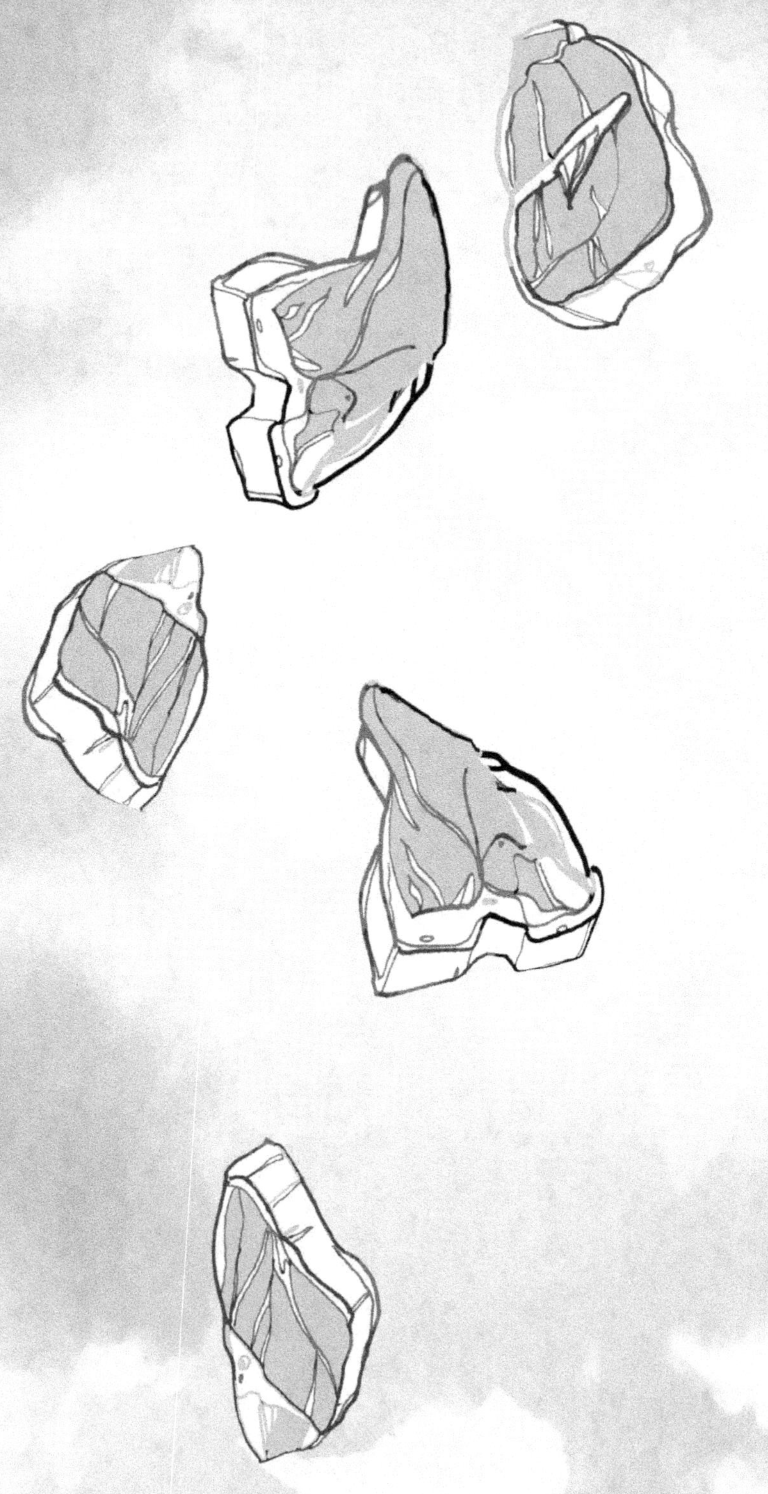

HIGH REWARD

Gabriel Craven & Mikayla Fawcett

Gabriel Craven is a comic artist and writer from Steveston, BC. His love of pulpy genre fiction runs hand in hand with his focus on small stories and everyday experiences.

Mikayla Fawcett is an interdisciplinary writer and artist. Before they finished typing this sentence, they went for a wetland wander, and then added three more buckets of yuck to the zombies featured in this comic.

For a different post-apocalyptic take from Mikayla and Gabriel, check out 'Afloat' in Pulp Literature Issue 17, Winter 2018.

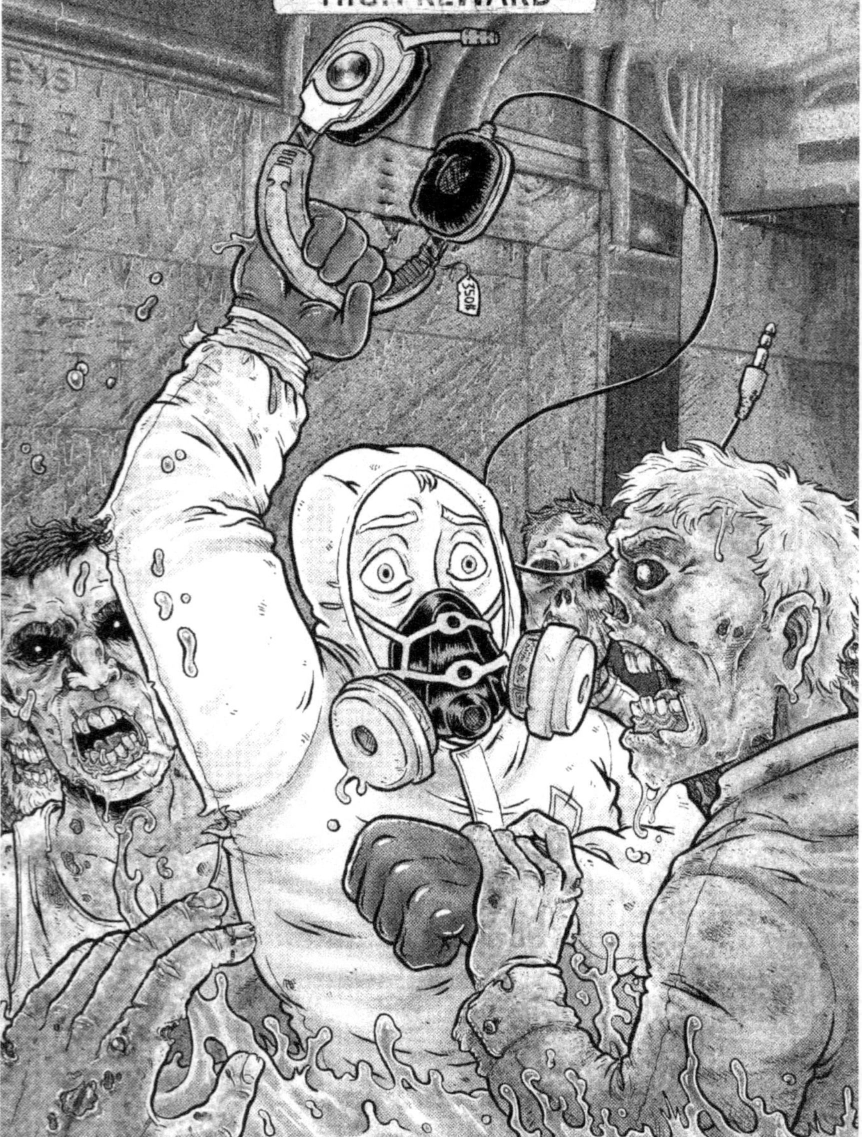
FINAL RESTORATION
HIGH REWARD

LORDS OF BONE WORLD
DREAD HOUSE
C'MON... C'MON...
LORDS OF BONE WORLD
DREAD HOUSE

Nicesw1ng
JameRPG we need CC GOGO!
JameRPG
okk
Nicesw1ng
Mic up dude your teamwork is shit today

GAME OVER BONEHEAD!

OH COME ON!

JAMIE PASCAL DAIGLE!
WE HAVE AN AGREEMENT. IF YOU'RE GOING TO PLAY YOUR GAMES, YOU KEEP IT QUIET!
SORRY, MOM!
IT JUST SLIPPED OUT.
GAME OVER BONEHE
IF YOUR TEENAGE GAMER RAGE BROUGHT AN UNDEAD NEIGHBOUR TO OUR HOUSE---
HNGUHH
WELL.
LORDS OF BONE WORLD
WOULD YOU LOOK AT THAT!
GAME'S OFF FOR THE NIGHT.
GO DEAL WITH HIM BEFORE HE ATTRACTS MORE TO THE YARD.
THEN GET READY FOR BED.
HRUUUGHH!

Uuhmm
mmuuh
UhMUH-h
WE'VE BOTH GOT WORK IN THE MORNING.

LOOK ALIVE, CREEP!

FFFwuh- BASH!

MORNING, MAN! SO, UH, HOW'RE YOU HOLDING UP?
MHRMM.
YEAH, THAT TRACKS.
YOUR GAME LAST NIGHT WAS HORRENDOUS.
SUMMER BBQ!
HAVE A BITE!
JULY 23rd
GO-FFEE!
FR
FR

DON'T I KNOW IT
I'VE BEEN PLAYING WITH THE SOUND OFF--
TRYING NOT TO ATTRACT ZED-HEADS
SO NOW I GET TO REALLY APPRECIATE THAT SOUND DESIGN.
I GET NO AUDIO CUES, NO ALERTS, NO VOICE CHAT, NO BEEDEE-BOODOO-- I DON'T EVEN GET THE DEATH JINGLE.
PLAYING WITHOUT SOUND IS LITERALLY KILLING ME.
YOU NEED SOME OMNI-DIRECTIONAL GAMER HEADPHONES, MAN.
GO-FFEE
YEAH, SURE. THAT SOUNDS NICE!
BUT BETWEEN MY TUITION PAYMENTS AND HELPING MOM OUT WITH THE RENT I DON'T REALLY HAVE ENOUGH LEFT OVER FROM MY PAY-CHEQUE TO JUST GO SHOPPING--
CERTAINLY NOT WHILE I'M STILL PART-TIME.
THAT'S 'CAUSE YOU ARE MAKING CHUMP CHANGE, MY FRIEND!
SUMMER BBQ HAVE A BITE JULY 23rd
WELL OBVIOUSLY
BUT I DON'T THINK THEY'RE GONNA GIVE ME A RAISE JUST SO I CAN KEEP UP WITH YOU IN LORDS OF BONEWORLD
AND I CAN'T DO FULL-TIME MID-SEMESTER, EITHER.

TCH!
IF IT'S JUST SOME EXTRA MAD MONEY YOU WANT, YOU DON'T NEED TO WAIT FOR YOUR NEXT RAISE --
--OR ADD ANY MORE HOURS TO YOUR WEEKLY GRIND.
SUMMER BBQ
HAVE A BITE JULY 23rd
WHEN YOU'RE AFTER HIGH-VALUE LOOT, YOU PARTAKE IN A HIGH-LEVEL QUEST.
JUST GET YOURSELF SET UP FOR HIGH-RISK JOBS.
HAZARD-PAY WORKS OUT TO TIME-AND-A-HALF.
HIGH-RISK JOBS?
THAT'S ALWAYS SOUNDED PRETTY TOUGH
SHIT-- WORK'S ALREADY TOUGH!
MIGHT AS WELL ENSURE IT'S WORTH IT.
HM. THAT DOES MAKE SENSE
SO! LET'S GET DOWN TO BRASS TACKS! I HEARD YOU WERE INTERESTED IN JOINING THE ENVIRONMENTAL TEAM?
OH, HE'S DOWN
TOO JUDGY
DON'T GET BITES
REPORT BITES!
JULY

WELL, I'M SORTA INTERESTED IN-
GLAD TO HEAR IT!
WE'RE ALWAYS HUNGRY FOR FRESH RECRUITS AROUND HERE!
WE'VE GOT A PRETTY HIGH TURN-OVER.
IN ANY CASE, WE'VE BEEN ABLE TO POLISH THE ORIENTATION PROCESS TO A SHINE!
SO! DO YOU HAVE ANY QUESTIONS FOR ME?
WELL...
I HEARD THAT THE ENVIRONMENTAL DEPARTMENT DEALS WITH "HIGH RISK" JOBS WHICH COUNT TOWARDS "HAZARD PAY"...?
AND I'M JUST NOT SURE WHAT ACTUALLY QUALIFIES AS "HIGH RISK."
I MEAN... ALL OUR TECHS ARE ALREADY OUT THERE FACING ZOMBIES ON A REGULAR BASIS.
YEP... ZOMBIES ARE EVERYWHERE THESE DAYS...
ON AND OFF THE JOB-SITE.
SOMETIMES IT SEEMS LIKE I'LL NEVER SEE THE END OF THE INCIDENT REPORTS...
...AND THOSE ARE JUST THE ONES THE TECHS ACTUALLY WRITE.
WHAT ROBBIE'S SAYING IS, ZOMBIES ARE TOO COMMON TO COUNT TOWARDS HAZARD PAY.
HAZARD PAY REQUESTS

ZOMBIES ARE CONSIDERATED MODERATE RISK--
AS PER THE NEW OPERATIONAL STANDARD.
OKAY...
SO WHAT COUNTS AS HIGH-RISK?
GOOD QUESTION! CHANCES ARE YOU'RE ALREADY ACQUAINTED WITH SOME OF THE STUFF YOU CAN EXPECT TO ENCOUNTER DURING HIGH-RISK WORK.
TOO JUDGY
DON'T GET BITES
REPORT BITES!
YOU GET ASBESTOS, SEWAGE, AND LEAD ABATEMENT
UNUSUALLY LARGE HORDES,
SILICA DUST,
JUDGY
NOVEL STRAIN ZOMBIE MUTANTS...
HIT
DON'T GET BITES
REPORT BITES!
AVOID
JULY
SORRY, WHAT WAS THAT?
SILLICA DUST.
IT'S FAR MORE DANGEROUS THAN MOST FOLKS GIVE IT CREDIT FOR.
IT MAY NOT THE STAR POWER OF ASBESTOS, BUT IT CAN DO TERRIBLE THINGS TO YOUR LUNGS.
TOO JUDGY
DON'T GET BITES
PPE

IT'S SIMPLE AS THIS: WHEN OTHER PEOPLE ARE TOO AFRAID TO TACKLE A REALLY NASTY JOB, WE GET CALLED IN --
AND WE GET IT DONE!
FR
YEAH!
AND WE GET IT DONE BY ADHERING TO RIGOROUS SAFETY PROTOCOLS!
JULY
JUDGY
GET
BEEDEE-BEEDEE-
GOOD MORNING! YOU'VE GOT ROBBIE! HOW CAN I HELP?
OHO! I SEE! JUST ONE MOMENT, PLEASE.
SAY, JAMIE! WHAT'D DISPATCH HAVE YOU DOING TODAY?!
JULY
UM-- UH-- HELPING SAM WITH A CONSTRUCTION CLEAN?!
FR
WELL, BOYS-- INFLUENZA FRIDAY IS UPON US ONCE AGAIN!
GREG HAS CALLED IN SICK
I'M GONNA GO AHEAD AND CALL THAT A TIMELY LEARNING OPPORTUNITY!
IF YOU'RE WILLING, WE'RE GONNA HAVE YOU JUMP ON IN!
REPORT BITES!

SO! YOU READY TO TANGO WITH THE NEW SUPER ZOMBIE?
YOU KNOW WHAT? I THINK I AM!
OPEN
PHONE REPAIR
CELL PHONE REPAIR
ALRIGHT! LET'S GET SUITED UP!
GUNK-RESISTANT HAZARD SHIT!
ANTI-CUT GLOVES!
FRESHLY FIT-TESTED HALF-MASK RESPIRATOR WITH FRESH FILTERS!
SAFETY GOGGLES!
NOW TO TAPE YOUR WRISTS.
NOT TOO TIGHT! YOU WANT A SEAL--
NOT A TOURNI-QUET!
LOOKING GOOD TO GO!
NOW ALL WE'VE GOT TO WORRY ABOUT IS SUFFOCATION, DEHYDRATION, HEAT EXHAUSTION, REDUCED FIELD OF VISION, AND NOT BEING ABLE TO COMMUNICATE CLEARLY IN THE EVENT OF AN EMERGENCY!

BIOHAZARD REMOVAL IN PROGRESS
...WORTH IT.
BONESTORM
LORDS OF BONE WORLD

THE SHEPHERDESS: EPIPHANY

JM Landels

JM Landels *is torn between travelling the world to teach writing and swordfighting, and never leaving her idyllic farm in Langley, BC. Her debut series, fantasy bestseller Allaigna's Song: Overture, and the sequels, Aria and Chorale, are available from Pulp Literature Press and most booksellers. You can follow her adventures with pen and sword at jmlandels.stiffbunnies.com.*

The Shepherdess: Epiphany

Previously in The Shepherdess …

Toinette, former shepherdess turned agent of the Silver Branch, has been reunited with her mistress, the Countess, at La Tectume, an apparently abandoned château fort in the Pyrénées that serves as a sanctuary for members of the order. Here she can recover from her harrowing journey, in which she walked from Paris to the Occitane and killed a man along the way.

I stayed at the Château Tectume for nearly ten months. During that time people came and went, including Madame and an assortment of women dignitaries. Of men, there were few. Henri was one and Luc another—though it seemed he was allowed to stay simply because he had arrived with Henri and me. Or perhaps 'allowed' is not the right word. 'Compelled' may be better.

I used the months to study. I was taught English, Spanish, Dutch, and Swedish here, to add to the Arabic, Latin, Greek, Hebrew, and German, I had begun learning at Versailles. I could not yet claim fluency in any of these, but I could read them and master a few words of conversation. For a shepherd from

St Geneviève, the fact I could read even my own language was a miracle. In addition to this, I studied alchemy and philosophy. The secrets learned from Madame, whom I still could not bring myself to call either Maeve — as she requested — or Catherine — as Henri called her — I may not tell you. Nor those I learned from mistress Aashvi. It worries me, and others of the Order, that this knowledge might die if not committed to paper. But we have all sworn an oath to store our arts in the fragile and temporary vessels of our flesh, and so we must be the books and tablets for the future to read. This account, written after most of the principal players are dead, is merely a way of transmitting my memories to you, my amanuensis, and you will burn it when my dictation ends.

I also learned something of the art of fencing from Madame, who insisted that if I was to be killing men with their own swords, I should at least do it properly. But I am not, nor ever shall be, la Maupin. I did learn to keep a slim knife in the top of my stocking, however, and between the bones of my stomacher I still guarded the lethal letter opener that had caused me so much trouble.

It was, in general, a remote, peaceful, and unhurried life at Tectume. Hot and dry in the summer, and windy beyond icy measure in the winter, but unbothered by visitors or further attacks. Until the day after the warm and quiet feast of Epiphany, when Michel de Foix rode his blown horse up to the château gates.

Michel was not the plumed courtier I'd met at Versailles. His plain cloak was travel-stained and worn, and the dark grey clothes might well have been the uniform of a Huguenot. He wore no wig, and his hair had grown long enough for a pigtail.

He stood in between the inner and outer bailey, hat in hand and shivering, while Madame debated whether to let him in or have Gwyn shoot him there.

Madame leaned over the portcullis balcony. "Well, my treacherous little spy, what shall I do with you?" she asked.

"A cup of ale and a hearth would be the minimum dictates of hospitality, my dear lady," said Michel.

"I have never trusted that little shit," growled Henri from behind Madame. "Even less now."

"I can hear you, Henri," called de Foix. "I've never trusted anyone, but that shouldn't impede the sharing of mutually beneficial information."

"You've never been known to give anything away for free, Michel," said Madame. "Surely you didn't ride all this way for a cup of beer. And the wine is much better than the beer in the *pays sûd* anyway."

"Could we please discuss this out of the wind, Maeve?" implored the man. "It's James," he said. "He has need of your skills."

"Henri," said Madame. "See to his horse. Please." Henri opened his mouth, no doubt to protest, but Madame's look silenced him. "And Toinette, have a bed made up on the second floor. Then meet me in the snug."

"And leave you alone with that villain?" Henri snorted.

"Quite alone." She patted his arm, then gave his elbow a small push toward the portcullis that was grinding upward to admit Michel de Foix and his horse.

"I'm not your stableman, de Foix," growled Henri. "Remember that."

Michel gave a half smile. "Appearances to the contrary. Noted," he said as he untied his saddlebags and scabbard. Encumbered by these items though he was, he still managed a graceful bow to Madame. "I am indebted and at your service, Comtesse."

Madame nodded and said, "Suivez," turning on her heel and leading the way across the yard.

Michel seemed not to recognize me, nor even take note of me—for who would when the countess stood near, plain dressed though she was?—and I was uninclined to reintroduce myself at that moment. I turned left and took the servants' stair to the chilly second floor to search out a more or less weatherproof room.

Our domicile of la Tectume vacillated between opulence and disrepair, depending on where one stood. From the valley it appeared a deserted ruin, and the villagers in the hamlet below were paid well not to let on otherwise. There were half a dozen charcoal burners scattered on the lower slopes of the mountain, whose kilns provided us with clean-burning fuel while disguising any errant smoke from our fires that might drift into the blue Pyrénéan sky.

To preserve the ruined appearance of the walls, the third and fourth storeys of the château were utterly abandoned to wind and birds, with a new makeshift roof patched together from the boards of the third level floor. But still, the windows of the second level were open to elements on the outer side, with smaller rooms constructed against the wall facing the inner courtyard. Modest and poorly lit, they were heated only by the hearths below.

Madame had instructed me to have a bed made up, but I could find no one at this late hour to whom to pass the task. I chose the room closest to the stair and spread fresh linens on the straw mattress that rested on wooden slats. I blew the dust out of a pewter jug and basin and left a tin chamber pot by the door. It was a far cry from Michel's usual habitation, I reckoned. And it was no doubt a statement from Madame that he not be welcomed on the first or ground floors.

By the time I reached the snug — Madame's winter office, half the size of the solar, and nestled in a leeward corner of the château — Michel was on his second cup of warm wine. He still stood before the hearth, shivering. His sodden cloak hung on the back of a chair, but he wore his coat, wet at the shoulders though it was. He held the tails tucked through one arm to expose his damp pantaloons to the fire. I wondered whether he had declined to sit or had not been invited.

We were not in the habit of court manners at la Tectume, but I felt the urge to bring the light and luxury of Versailles into the miserable form of de Foix and the unhappy face of my mistress. So I gave my deepest, slowest curtsy, worthy of the Royal Chamber itself. "Madame la Comtesse, Chevalier. There is a room prepared on the second floor. Shall I bring a repast here or there?" For the sake of the shivering Michel, I hoped Madame would allow him to warm himself in the snug before exiling him to the draughty second floor.

"Neither, Toinette. The kitchen is warmer than either by far, and our talk here is done for now."

"Toinette?" Michel's face broke into a smile as radiant as the gilded suns that decorated Versailles. He turned a leg and gave a sweeping bow that momentarily blocked the heat with his coat tails. "Ma petite 'soeur', forgive me. Dressed in home-spun, I thought you were merely some unusually beautiful serving wench."

I had spent less than a year at Versailles, but I could smell false flattery at twice the distance. "You thought no such thing, 'mon frère'," I corrected. "You failed to notice me entirely." Though I enjoyed making the man squirm, I still felt too much sympathy for his wretched state to let him suffer more. "And why should you? You would hardly expect to find, so close to your home, the ingénue we passed off as your sister at Versailles." Part of my time here at the château had been spent studying roll after roll of maps, from every corner of the continent but particularly from our own royaume. And so I knew, as a matter of course, that Michel's family seat of Foix was a three-day ride due west of La Tectume. Not that I'd been there — I seldom left the mountaintop — but I let him think I had. "Let me show you to the kitchens."

Madame's eyes, as I took leave of the snug, said 'return here forthwith'.

I had many questions I wanted to ask Michel, but none I knew how to phrase without first consulting with Madame. Michel filled the silence with his own questions instead.

"Last I'd heard, the Countess had left her household behind in Versailles," he began as he tucked a soggy, importunate arm through mine. "Were my efforts at establishing you not enough to keep you there?"

"Not at all. Your name and introductions opened many a door for me. Most of which I assume remain open. I chose to follow my mistress here."

"Maeve usually prefers to keep her households separate. It's a mark of her favour that she chose to bring you."

"I hope to prove worthy of that favour," I replied, omitting that I'd followed her unbidden, at a remove of two months, and at the cost of much shoe leather and some spilled blood. "She does not seem especially pleased with your arrival," I ventured, and then softened the insult with "or perhaps with the news you brought."

"I don't flatter myself that she'd be happy with my news, or with me," he said with a shrug. "Mon Dieu, that smells better than all the perfumes in Versailles," he announced, changing the topic of conversation as we reached the door to the kitchen.

I left Michel gorging himself on Salmana's excellent cooking, and took two bowls of pigeon stew back to the snug for myself and Madame.

With my belly full of stew and new worries, I bade Madame good night and took our dishes down to the kitchen. Even though I was nominally her femme de chambre, here at la Tectume we didn't stand on ceremony. She would undress herself, braid her own hair, and leave the lamp turned low for me to find my way back later that night. Not to a separate room or even a cot in hers, for we shared the heavy-curtained bed, conserving both heat and linens. Normally I would read to her: from Descartes, More, and de Gournay on nights when she was in a modern mood; Sappho, Hypatia, and Homer when she wanted me to improve my Greek; and Rabelais, Shakespeare, Pascal, and Molière when she wanted to be entertained. But tonight she begged an early sleep on account of a kindling headache. I felt one sparking in my temples as well, but had too much to ponder to crawl into bed yet.

Once I'd washed our dishes, I retrieved a warming pan from the overhead rack and filled it with coals from the hearth. But instead of taking it to our bed, which would be warm already from Madame's presence, I took the extra set of stairs to the second floor. I trusted Salmana had shown Michel his room, and indeed, a light shone from beneath the ill-fitting door. I knocked and entered without waiting for a reply.

"Toinette!" exclaimed Michel, who was hanging his pantaloons beside his surcoat on pegs stuck into the unplastered wall. "Were you hoping to catch me en déshabille?"

"You have on your shirt, hose, and braies. I doubt you'll be removing those in this temperature, unless you were hoping—vainly—that Salmana might keep you company tonight."

He put a hand to his chest. "You wound me, mademoiselle, to think I would take advantage of the château's servants. Though a warm body next to me would be welcome indeed …" he raised a questioning eyebrow.

"You'll have to make do with this." I crossed the small room in a single stride and tucked the warming pan between the sheets on his bed. "It would hardly be appropriate to share a bed with your 'sister'."

"Alas, the day I adopted you as ma petite soeur. Is it a guise you still use?"

"Here in la Tectume, no. But I will no doubt have to return to Versailles at some point, and I feel it's best not to mar the outlines of the character."

"Then I thank you for the coals, mademoiselle." He gave one of his signature bows, made only slightly less impressive by the fact he was in his underclothes.

I remained standing between him and the pallet. "Why are you here?" I demanded. Madame had told me what we must do, but not why, and I wanted greater understanding.

"Because I haven't been invited to the main floors … but that's not what you are asking, is it?" Without his wig and his fine clothes, Michel seemed less inclined to the parry-riposte of court dialogue. "You are new to this métier, but you must know that you'll find no ready answers for the asking from such as us."

Flattered as I was by my inclusion in the unspoken profession of 'spy', I was not ready to release my ingénue status yet. I folded my legs to sit on the pallet and patted the space beside me, which was now warm from the spreading heat of the chauffe-lit. "Come, Michel, sit and help me understand."

He let out a long-suffering sigh. "If you want to chat, we'll chat, but first get off the bed. Il fait un froid de canard in here."

I rose, and he removed the top blanket of the bed, settling down next to the lump of the warming pan beneath the sheet. He put the blanket around his shoulders and held open one side for me to sit next to him.

I took the offered end of the blanket and tucked it around him, sealing him in with the warming pan.

"I'm dressed for this temperature," I said as I settled next to his bundled figure. Fierce as the mountain winds were, I found them easier to withstand than the damp winter chill that covers the backs of the sheep with wet snow in marshy St Geneviève. Still, this close to the floor I could feel the draught that forced its way beneath the ill-fitting door like a cold knife. I abandoned my sabots and tucked my feet beneath my skirts. "Don't worry," I said. "I won't pry any secrets from your lips."

"Nor kisses neither, I suppose?" he said wistfully.

"I require advice. And perhaps a tale. How did you become a spy?"

He winced at a question too blunt for courtly manners. "That, Toinette, is a word that should pass your lips seldom, if ever."

"It is what you are, is it not?"

"In the courts of the Sun King and his counterparts in England, Holland, and Spain, there are few that could not lay claim to such an appellation."

"Ah, but on an amateur or professional level?"

He inclined his head. "You have me there, mademoiselle. But I am no more or less a professional than your own mistress."

"Indeed." But I knew Madame's history, and how her entire identity was of necessity a falsehood. "But how did you become so, Chevalier?"

He leaned out of his blanket tent and pulled his saddlebag close to the bed, rummaging in it as he spoke. "Like you, I stumbled into it. It was partly being in the wrong—or perhaps right—place at the right or wrong time. When someone higher in the social hierarchy asks a favour, one doesn't refuse. And then one has knowledge that is dangerous, and only more knowledge can counter that danger. At some point one must commit and take a side, if only for a while, and hope the patronage of those who pay your bills can protect you." He procured a silver flask from the saddlebag and offered it to me. "Drink?"

Henri would have taken a drink first and only offered the flask as an afterthought, if at all. I took the flask, unstoppered it, and sniffed. Armagnac. Whose complex aromas could hide any number of unhealthy additives. I handed it back. "Thank you, but brandy does my head no good."

He took it back with a smile and a nod. "Very sage, mademoiselle." He drank from the flask and put it on the floor between us. "If you change your mind."

I had no reason to suspect Michel would poison me, but this felt like a test. I would not be distracted. "And who is it that protects you? And from whom?"

"Those questions are too direct, and I believe you know it." His hand stole out from the blanket again, but this time he rested it on mine. "I want to help you, mademoiselle. Ask a different question."

"Then tell me about your — 'our' — family. And the home I allegedly come from. For it's a story I may have to support at some point."

The candle was near guttering and the chauffe-lit gone cold by the time I left Michel's room. It was not so much a history he told me, but one we constructed together. It went something like this:

"In my seventh year, I began riding that rascally pony Carbonette —"

"And who did I ride?"

"You were a babe-in-arms."

"But later, when I was old enough to ride?"

"Carbonette outlived Baillet, my next horse, so no doubt you were put on that little demoness Carbon."

"And that harrowing experience is surely why I never learned to ride."

Or:

"Before I left for court, I secretly married my childhood sweetheart, Sophie."

"Why secretly?"

"She was a milliner's daughter. Hardly a suitable match."

"Was she with child?"

"Not that I know of. She died before I returned. Smallpox."

"I am sorry." I put my hand on top of the blanket under which his rested.

He shook his head. "Thank you. We were sweethearts, but that's not why I married her. It was to save her from being wed to a widowed merchant thrice her age." There was a long pause. "Had she married him, she may have lived."

There was more there, but I felt a wall forming between us. I looked for a way around. "Were we friends?"

"Yes. The best of friends."

I knew then. "Your real sister," I said, easing a toe past the wall. "Where is she now?"

He took a swig from his flask. "In the ground next to the convent that my parents sent her to." There was no fictitious 'our' accompanying 'parents' this time. "Along with half a dozen other sisters of the order. But my father had disowned her before that. You'd do well to never meet the evil bastard, Toinette."

After that, he refused to talk any more of home but instead told me gay anecdotes from court life, many of which I'd heard before. It was interesting to note which details stayed firm and which altered with the telling. But there were gaps. I counted them on my fingers, like missing sheep.

"Oh, you don't want to hear about my time in England, Toinette. It is a dreary place, with bad weather and worse cuisine. For all the reputed excesses of the restored monarch, there remains a dour puritan streak that lies on the populace like mizzling fog. The court of Charles holds but a weak candle to that of our Sun King."

Then why, I thought, *do you spy for him?* Out loud I said, as if it were no question, "But that was where you met James."

"His Grace, the Duke of York? No, I met the English king's younger brother when he was in exile here in France."

"And why does he have need of Madame?"

Michel paused for less than a heartbeat in his reply, but I felt a sudden tension in his shoulders through the blanket. "What makes you think he does?"

"You said to her, when you arrived, 'James has need of you.'"

"Ah. There are many Jameses in the world, Toinette. Almost as many as there are Louis and Louises."

It was a reasonable answer, but I felt my query had struck near the mark, nonetheless. "Which one has need of her, then?"

"That, you will have to ask her."

I felt closer to Michel after our long evening, but no closer to fully trusting him. There were areas, especially those that touched the shores of England, where his answers floated on shifting tides. Such was his — and, I allowed, our — profession. Would I ever, having embarked in this world, trust anyone not bearing a silver branch imprinted on their skin?

I closed the door to Madame's chamber as quietly as I could and took a moment to add a piece of twisted olive wood to the smouldering hearth. Despite my efforts not to wake her, Madame rolled over when I slipped past the bed's curtains and slid my stockinged feet beneath the covers.

"You smell of Michel," she murmured, her voice thick with sleep. "Were you having a wee tryst? You'll make Luc furious with envy."

"Luc? What claim has he on jealousy? And no, Madame, I have no interest in Michel beyond what rests between his ears. I spent several hours trying to fill in his *histoire* since we saw him last."

"Without apprising him of yours, of course." She yawned.

"Mais bien sûr."

"And had you any luck?"

"We talked of his further distant past instead. He had a real sister, it seems."

She reached over and grasped my hand. "Are you regretting adopting the guise of a shade?"

I shook my head, though she couldn't see me in the velvet dark. "No. I think it may give him a modicum more feeling towards me than he might otherwise have, and that is always an advantage." I wanted to mull that more before I discussed it with anyone, even Madame. "How is your headache?"

"Nearly gone."

"Then may I ask you about this James, who has such need of you that we must shift ourselves from our comfortable rest here?"

I could feel her smile despite the dark. "You learned more than family history from Michel, then. Brava. But it is time to return to court, regardless. His Majesty does not tolerate long absences from Versailles, and I am stretching the bounds of his indulgence as is."

I would not be deflected. "Who is James? It's an English name."

"And a Scottish, and an Irish one."

"*Seamus, is it then?*" I asked in Gaelic.

"Your accent is still appalling, ma petite, but it is improving. No, not a Seamus. Just an Englishman I've had dealings with in the past. But I can't invite him here, so we'll meet him in Narbonne and continue on from there to Paris and Versailles."

There was more she wasn't saying, but there always was. I needed to grow comfortable with the truth that I would not ever know everything. Now that I had some knowledge of the world, my hunger for more was insatiable.

"I will be sad to leave here." I interlaced my fingers with hers—a familiarity that would never be acceptable between a mistress and her servant once we were back in society. "May we make one more stop along the way?"

"Where?"

"St Geneviève. It has been too long since I saw my mother and sisters."

"But of course, ma chère." She stroked my hair. "We must not forget our mothers and sisters." She left a feather-light kiss, scented with hyssop and cloves, upon my lips. "Bonne nuit, Toinette. We ride tomorrow."

§

We return to the world of The Shepherdess *in Pulp Literature Issue 44, Autumn 2024. To catch up on Toinette's adventures till now, check out even numbers of PL starting with Issue 24, Autumn 2019.*

Allaigna's Song
Overture
JM Landels
AMAZON #1 BESTSELLER
Allaigna's Song
Aria
JM Landels

THE ARTISTS

Mel Anastasiou
Cover artist, Red Planet Raygunne and the Answer to Everything,
in-house illustrator
Mel Anastasiou loves drawing for *Pulp Literature* because she loves the stories she illustrates. She draws in black and white, working from imagination and inspired by details from Renaissance compositions. You can find illustrations, writing tips, and news about her books and novellas at melanastasiou. wordpress.com, and see more of her artwork on Facebook at Bird and Branch Artwork.

For the cover of Issue 42 — Mel's favourite number, obviously — we welcome back our interstellar explorer, Raygunne, first seen in the title page of Issue 3, and then again in Issues 22 and 34. She's about to set foot on the Red Planet, hoping she'll discover the answer to everything.

Gabriel Craven and Mikayla Fawcett
Creators, 'High Reward'
'High Reward' is a short story from *Final Restoration*, Gabriel and Mikayla's series about the zombie-fighting blue-collar workers at a restoration company of the same name. It started in 2016 as a series of strips poking fun at zombie apocalypse escapism fantasies where the characters break out of their mundane lives and become post-apocalyptic badasses. What if zombies

attacked, and instead of the full-societal reset, most of us went back to business as usual? Drawing from working experience in the restoration industry, the creators felt that zombies made a natural addition to the roster of job site hazards. There's a life-threatening pandemic out there, and you've still got to make rent somehow. Absurd? Sure. But what can you do?

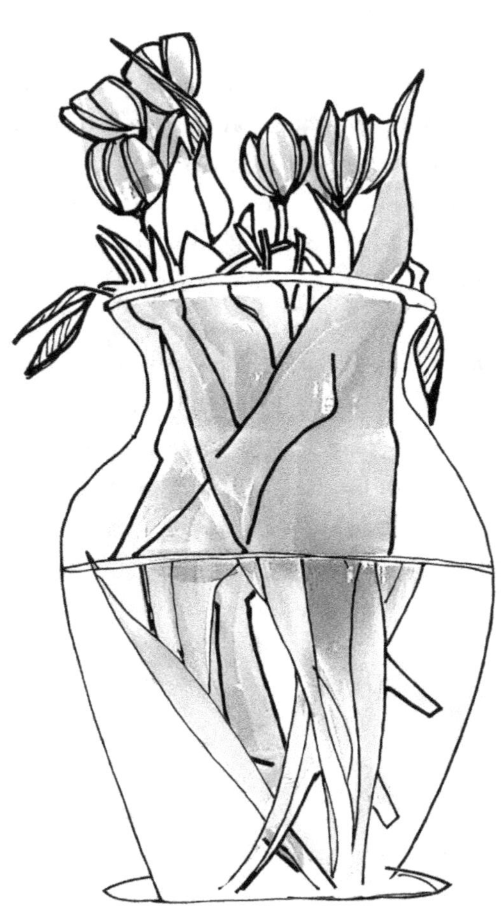

HALL OF FAME

*These are the heroes — the Patrons and Pulp Literati whose monthly support
helped bring you this issue. Please lift your glasses and give them a rousing cheer!*

The Brewers
Dana Tye Rally

The Innkeepers
Andrea Kepple
David Jensen
Ev Bishop
Gillian Gardiner
Kevin Harris
Lorna Ens
Mark Francis
Richard Ohnemus
Robin McGillveray
Susan Jackson

The Cicerones
Jennifer Sommersby
Roger & Anne Anastasiou

The Bartenders
Alana Krider
Andrea Kirkham
Anna Belkine
April DC
Benjamin Johnson
Bjarne Hansen
Brighton Hugg

Bryan Moose
Chris Olee
Dave Wayne
Deepthi Atukorala
Ernst Pulido
Finnian Burnett
Fran Scannell
James Carlino
Jennifer Getsinger
Jillian Shoichet
John Olley
K Anastasiou
Katherine Derbyshire
Katriona Greenmoor
kc dyer
KT Wagner
Leny Wagner
Lin & John Richardson
Margaret Elliott
Margot Landels
Margot Spronk
Maureen Cooke
Megan Shaw
Michelle Balfour
Mike Sylvester
Peter Halasz
Rapscallion

Richard Gropp
Ron Graves
Scott F Gray
Scott Carrothers
Shannon Saunders
Star
Suzanne Philip
Venasa Simpson

The Regulars
Adam Fout
Akemi Art
Andy W
BC
Catherine Levinson
Charity Tahmaseb
David Perlmutter
James Gotaas
Jenny Blackford
Marilyn Holt
Marta Salek
Meredith Frazier
Paul Anguiano
Rhea Rose
Rina Piccolo
Sonia Brock
Vera

*If you would like to join the ranks of these worthies, you can become a patron
on Patreon at patreon.com/pulplit or join the Pulp Literati through our website
at pulpliterature.com/join-pulp-literati/.*

Out of the fires of a Caribbean slave revolt, shipwrecked on the jungle coast of 16th-century Ecuador, an educated slave, a shaman, and a monk hunted by the Inquisition fight for freedom against the might of Imperial Spain.

Dive into an epic slipstream novel of intrigue and adventure from fantasy author Matthew Hughes, the writer George R.R. Martin calls 'criminally underrated,' and Robert J. Sawyer says is 'a towering talent.'

'A triumph!' - Cecelia Holland
'Sensational' - Candas Jane Dorsey

pulpliterature.com
Fantastic Fresh Fiction!

PULP
Literature

IGNITE YOUR IMAGINATION

30 yrs of award-winning sci-fi and fantasy

WWW.ONSPEC.CA

In search of a writing community?

Join today!

The Federation of BC Writers is here for you!

- ☑ Workshops/ Webinars
- ☑ Contests
- ☑ Readings
- ☑ Articles

- ☑ Networking
- ☑ Discount Membership for for Students and Seniors

- ☑ Digital Writing Circles
- ☑ Find Inspiration & more!

bcwriters.ca/Join

MARKETPLACE

Books

Advent *by Michael Kamakana* • We thought we knew what the aliens wanted. Think again. • pulpliterature.com/advent

Allaigna's Song: Chorale *by JM Landels* The long-awaited conclusion to the bestselling *Allaigna's Song* trilogy. • pulpliterature.com/allaignas-song

The Extra: A Monument Studios Mystery *by Mel Anastasiou* • Extra Frankie Ray gets her big break on the Silver Screen, until murder steals the scene. • pulpliterature. com/the-extra

The Labours of Mrs Stella Ryman: Further Fairmount Mysteries *by Mel Anastasiou* • Trapped in a down-at-the-heels care home. You'd be cranky too. • pulpliterature.com/stella-ryman-and-the-fairmount-manor-mysteries

What the Wind Brings *by Matthew Hughes* • Winner of the 2020 Endeavour Award • pulpliterature.com/product-category/novels/matthew-hughes

The Writer's Boon Companion *by Mel Anastasiou* • Thirty Days Towards an Extraordinary Volume • pulpliterature.com/subscribe/the-bookstore

Bookstores

Russell Books • 100-747 Fort St, Victoria, BC • russellbooks.com

Western Sky Books • 2132-2850 Shaughnessy St, Port Coquitlam, BC V3C 6K5 • 604-461-5602 • store.westernskybooks.com

White Dwarf / Dead Write Books • 3715 10th Ave W, Vancouver, BC V6R 2G5 • 604-228-8223 • whitedwarf@deadwrite.com

Conferences & Events

When Words Collide • August 10-12, 2024 Calgary, AB • whenwordscollide.org

Wine Country Writers' Festival • 27-29 September, 2024 winecountrywriters-festival.ca

Surrey International Writers' Conference October 2024 • siwc.ca

Printing & Publishing

First Choice Books/Victoria Bindery Book printing & binding • graphic design • eBooks • marketing materials 1-800-957-0561 • firstchoicebooks.ca

Writing Resources

Dreamers Creative Writing • Workshops, residencies, contests & more! • www.dreamerswriting.com

Magazines

Amazing Stories · Back in print! amazingstories.com

The Digest Enthusiast · Digests past & present plus new genre fiction larquepress.com

EVENT Magazine · Poetry & prose eventmagazine.ca

Geist · Ideas + Culture · Made in Canada · geist.com

Mystery Weekly Magazine · The cutting edge of short mystery fiction www.mysteryweekly.com

Neo-opsis · Canadian magazine of science fiction based in Victoria, BC · neo-opsis.ca

OnSpec · The Canadian magazine of the fantastic · onspecmag.wordpress.com

Polar Borealis · Paying market for new Canadian SF&F writers & artists · polarborealis.ca

Room Magazine · Literature, Art & Feminism since 1975 · roommagazine.com

CONTESTS

Pulp Literature runs five annual contests for poetry, flash fiction, and short stories. For contest guidelines, prizes, and entry fees, see pulpliterature.com/contests.

The Magpie Award for Poetry
Contest opens: 1 March 2024
Deadline: 15 April 2024
Winner notified: 15 May 2024
Winner published: Issue 44, Autumn 2024
Prize: $500

The Hummingbird Flash Fiction Prize
Contest opens: 1 May 2024
Deadline: 15 June 2024
Winner notified: 15 July 2024
Winner published: Issue 45, Winter 2025
Prize: $300

The Raven Short Story Contest
Contest opens: 1 September 2024
Deadline: 15 October 2024
Winner notified: 15 November 2024
Winner published: Issue 46, Spring 2025
Prize: $300

The Kingfisher Poetry Prize
Contest opens: 1 October 2024
Deadline: 15 November 2024
Winner notified: 15 December 2024
Winner published: Issue 46, Spring 2025
Prize: $300

The Bumblebee Flash Fiction Contest
Contest opens: 1 January 2025
Deadline: 15 February 2025
Winner notified: 15 March 2025
Winner published: Issue 47, Summer 2025
Prize: $300

EVENT

36th ANNUAL NON-FICTION CONTEST

INCREASED CASH PRIZES
$1,500 • $1,000 • $500

OCTOBER 15

Non-Fiction Contest winners feature in every volume since 1989 and have received recognition from the Canadian Magazine Awards, National Magazine Awards and Best Canadian Essays. All entries considered for publication. Entry fee of $34.95 includes a one-year subscription. We encourage writers from diverse backgrounds and experience levels to submit their work.

eventmagazine.ca

Arc's Poem of the Year
wins a grand prize of
$5,000

How to Submit: Enter your poem(s) thru Submittable or via snail mail to PO Box 81060, Ottawa, Ontario, K1P 1B1

Entry Fee: $40 CAD for 1 or 2 poems (or up to 3 poems before the Early Bird deadline), includes a one-year subscription* to *Arc Poetry Magazine*. Additional entries are $5 CAD per poem.

Early Bird Deadline: December 31, 2023
Final Deadline: February 1, 2024

Find more details online at arcpoetry.ca/contests

*one-year subscriptions only available to entrants in Canada. Entrants in the US will receive 2 issues, entrants outside of Canda and the US will receive 1 issue

ARC **POETRY**

$\mathcal{B}$ECOME A PATRON OF PULP LITERATURE

By supporting *Pulp Literature* on Patreon with $2 or more per month, you will be laying the foundation for a secure future for the magazine, as well as ensuring that you never miss an issue! Your subscription includes four big issues of short stories, novellas, poetry, comics, and novel excerpts, delivered to your door or electronic mailbox each year. **Find us at patreon.com/pulplit**

If you prefer to subscribe through our website, go to pulpliterature. com/subscribe.

Or you can send a cheque with the form below to
Subscriptions, Pulp Literature Press, 21955 16 Ave, Langley BC, V2Z 1K5, Canada

Don't miss an issue!

- ❑ **Send me 2 years (8 issues) at the special rate of $110** (save $34)*
- ❑ **Send me 1 year (4 issues) for $60** (save $12)*
- ❑ **Send me 2 years of digital issues for $35** (save $12.92)
- ❑ **Send me 1 year of digital issues for $20** (save $3.96)

Name: ____

Address: ____

City: ________________________________ Prov. / State: _________

Postal code: _______________ Country: ____________________

Email: ____

❑	Payment enclosed	Make cheques payable in Canadian funds to Pulp Literature Press. Include email address for digital editions and Paypal billing, or subscribe at www.pulpliterature.com/subscribe.
❑	Bill me	
❑	New	*for postage outside Canada add $20 per year in North America or $32 per year overseas.
❑	Renewal